THE DOOMSDAY BULLET

THE DOOMSDAY BULLET

RAY HOGAN

DOUBLEDAY & COMPANY, INC.
GARDEN CITY, NEW YORK
1981

Library of Congress Cataloging in Publication Data

Hogan, Ray, 1908–
The doomsday bullet.

I. Title.
PS3558.03473D6   813'.54
ISBN: 0-385-17554-X
Library of Congress Catalog Card Number 80-2839

for

JESSICA AND JON HOGAN

THE DOOMSDAY BULLET

CHAPTER 1

Marshal John Rye drew his horse to a stop, dismounted, and heaved a sigh of relief as his aching leg and back muscles responded gratefully to the change. He had been in the saddle since well before first light, pushing hard the big chestnut gelding he was riding, and the stocky, gray pack horse trailing at the end of a lead rope.

Drawing a stogie from the leather case in his shirt pocket, he bit off the end and fired a match with a thumbnail. Touching the flame to the tip of the black weed, he puffed it into life as he stared out across the vast New Mexico flats and low hills. Crisscross, the troubled town for which he was heading, could not be far now.

Rye vaguely recalled a description of the place—a small, active settlement at the intersection of several roads, such junction being the basis for its singular but logical name. The town was in trouble; its lawman, a sheriff named Charley Gaskol, had been murdered, and the lawless element had taken over, according to word received by Rye from his superiors. He was ordered to go there, take charge, restore law and order, and maintain such until the territorial governor could find a replacement for Gaskol. Because of certain complications which he would better understand once he arrived there, the job could be expected to take anywhere from a few days to a couple of weeks or even longer; regardless, he was to remain on the job, and leave only when the new lawman put in his appearance.

Rye, flat-crowned hat tipped forward to shade his eyes from the mid-morning sun, let his glance sweep the broad land before him appraisingly. Ahead lay the rugged, almost bleak grandeur that was New Mexico; to his left, the east, was the Oklahoma Strip—the Panhandle—the No Man's Land so favored by outlaws because it lay unclaimed by surrounding states and territories, and law was nonexistent. Behind him, to the north, were the arid slopes of Colorado; farther on, a bit to the west, were the great, towering hills with their sky-piercing peaks.

He had been in Montana when the urgent directive to head for Crisscross had reached him. There had been few details given, simply the order to drop whatever he was doing, and ride out immediately. Rye had followed instructions, and now with nearly two weeks of travel behind him, was savoring the realization that the long ride was almost over.

The lawman, taking his ease, continued to study the country through half-closed seemingly colorless eyes. His black leather vest was coated with dust, and his gray shirt was sweat-stained. Cord pants showing the signs of constant wear, knee-high, stovepipe boots badly scarred, he nevertheless gave the appearance of what he was: a deadly, violent man, intense, inscrutable and the very personification of the law he believed in—the law he would go to any length to uphold. There was no question why he was known as the Doomsday Marshal to friend and foe alike.

Carrying a special lawman's commission said to have

been authorized and signed by President Rutherford B. Hayes, he was an efficient specialist in his profession, a superior man dispatched to take over and handle a specific problem that others had failed—or feared—to confront. That he was ruthless, seemingly invincible and altogether independent was conceded by all with whom he dealt, and because of such, an aura of hostility and isolation surrounded him, depriving him of close friends and affording him merely acquaintances.

Spring had not yet fully given way to summer and its often fierce heat, and the land was still gentle with a carpet of range grass extending to all directions as far as the eye could see. Here and there vivid splashes of wildflowers—paintbrush, butterfly weed, scarlet penstemon, coral globemallow and others—broke the sameness of the hills and plains.

Squat juniper trees, called desert cedars by some, dotted the countryside, along with rose-blossomed cholla cactus, and their kinsmen, yellow-flowered prickly pear. In the deep arroyos, cottonwoods spread thickly leafed limbs.

Off to his left a village of prairie dogs was observing him with alert curiosity, just as had other wild dwellers of the hills and plains—coyotes, rabbits, deer and a lone pair of white-flagged antelopes, survivors of once countless herds. Birds had been plentiful also during the long journey, especially yellow-throated horned larks, which continually flung themselves up into the brilliant sky at his approach.

It had been a lengthy ride made less tedious by his appreciation of the stark beauty of the land across which he had ridden, and despite the numerous times he had journeyed back and forth across the frontier in general, he never wearied of seeing it. Such was probably the one soft spot in John Rye's hard makeup—his vulnerability to the majestic, often delicate, quality of the country. Perhaps it was that facet of his composition that made him a relentless foe of all outlaws; to him they were the enemy of the law, and therefore of the decent people who would, by their labors, further the land's beauty and production.

Turning, Rye moved to the gray and examined the packsaddle and its load. All was yet secure. Stepping then to the chestnut, he swung back into the saddle, his broad hand going automatically and without conscious thought to the forty-five Colt resting in its low-cut holster on his hip. Reassured of its presence, his fingers then sought the short-barreled shotgun in the boot slung from the hull, accounting for it also. It was a ritual continually followed at such times, for it represented the difference between life and death to him, and he was careful never to separate himself from at least one of the weapons regardless of circumstances.

Finding all to his liking, John Rye again swept the country ahead with a probing glance. According to information given him, Crisscross would lie somewhere beyond the rolling hills to the southeast, but he had never been in that specific part of the area before, always having passed farther west, so he could not be exactly certain where the settlement would be.

His consideration faltered. A frown came to his dark, unshaven face. Etched against the cloudless sky, off to his left, a dozen vultures were lazily circling, intent on something off the trail.

Taking up the chestnut's lines, eyes fixed on the broad-winged scavengers, the lawman put the big gelding into motion. Likely it was some animal—or several to attract so many buzzards—dead or dying that had drawn the birds' grisly attention, but he had best look into it. It could be a party of pilgrims in trouble, victims of an accident or of one of the scattered bands of roving Arapahoes or Kiowas that were reported to be plaguing this particular section of the land. At any rate, he'd take a few minutes and investigate—that much every man owed a fellow traveler.

A half hour later Rye again drew to a halt, this time on the lip of a fairly deep swale. A hardness came into his pale eyes and his long lips tightened into a grim line. Several bodies—five or six at least, and as many horses—lay dead in the bright sunshine near the center of the grassy depression a short distance from the trail. The lawman was no stranger to death in its many forms, but the sight of what appeared to be wholesale slaughter jarred him solidly, and momentarily sent shock waves of horror through him. Then, raking the chestnut with his spurs, he rode down into the swale for a closer look.

CHAPTER 2

Soldiers . . . cavalrymen . . . Rye spotted uniforms, well-coated with dust and matted dirt, when he drew nearer. The men lay close to their horses, as if they had fallen together. Indians? Rye gave that thought, dismissed the possibility; a hunting party of warriors would not have killed the horses.

Halting a few yards from the scene, Rye had a thorough look at the surrounding area. The soldiers had not been dead long, it appeared, the ambush or whatever had happened probably taking place that previous day or night. A dense stand of sagebrush in a ragged wash lay a dozen yards on beyond the soldiers, and the ambushers, if that's what it had been, likely had lain in wait there.

Convinced there was no one else nearby, ignoring the hordes of buzzing flies, the lawman rode in close and dismounted.

"Friend—"

At the sound of the word, labored and at low breath, Rye whirled. One of the soldiers was alive—an elderly man wearing the chevrons of a top sergeant. Taking the canteen from his saddle, Rye knelt beside the non-com.

Holding the container to the man's lips, the marshal forced a drink into his throat. Then, as the soldier grasped the canteen greedily, Rye relinquished his grip. Shading the sergeant's face with his own hat, he leaned back.

"What the hell happened?"

The soldier let the canteen lower to one side, stirred wearily. "Bushwhacked—about a half a dozen men. They got the wagon."

Rye frowned, glanced about. Only then did he see the wide imprints made by iron-tired wheels on the sun-baked turf.

"Something special about the wagon?"

The sergeant stirred again. "Plenty, mister—"

"Name's John Rye, I'm a special U.S. marshal."

"Good—glad to hear that. I'm Exter—Henry Exter. Had a squad from Fort Churchill, Nevada. We was delivering gold."

"Gold?" Rye echoed. "What the devil was the Army doing delivering gold?"

"Was new double eagles—Carson City mint. Was taking them to Fort Union—two hundred thousand dollars' worth."

Payroll and expense money to maintain the New Mexico post, Rye guessed. Then, "Seems like a small escort for that much money."

"Done it that way a'purpose. Been some holdups before. This time they fixed the wagon with a false bottom, then loaded it with regular supplies—medicine, stuff like—like that." Exter paused, took another long swallow of water, and continued, his voice low and faltering.

"Was somebody at—at the mint passed the word we was carrying gold. We had the wagon fixed so's nobody would know, a real little chest, sort of—of flat that we put under the false bottom of the wagon bed. Somebody had to have talked—told them bushwhackers about it—'cause they'd a'never knowed that chest was hid there, otherwise. And we took only one squad of men—so's not to draw no attention. Wanted it to look like just some regular patrol."

"But the outlaws were waiting for you in that draw yonder all the same. Had been tipped off, that's sure."

Exter nodded weakly. "We never knowed what hit us. One minute—one minute we was riding along cozy as you please with Silverman driving the wagon—had his horse tied on behind—we aimed to leave the wagon at Union. Next—next thing I knowed we was in a hail of bullets. . . . You mind if I have another swig of that water, Marshal?"

"No, help yourself," Rye said. "Got a pint of whiskey in my saddlebags—"

Exter managed a tight smile, lowered the canteen. "Lord, a shot of redeye right now sure would ease my innards a'plenty!"

The lawman quickly obtained the liquor. Pulling the cork, he placed the bottle in the sergeant's hands and waited while the man had a long swallow.

"That helps—helps a'plenty," Exter said, returning the bottle. "Mighty thankful you—you come along. Been laying here watching them damned buzzards going round and round, getting close—and thinking—thinking about them chewing—on me and the boys. Was hoping—maybe I was even praying—somebody'd show up—before they—them damn birds got to me."

"When did that bunch of outlaws jump you?" Rye asked, with an upward glance at the circling buzzards.

"Late yesterday it was—about—about a hour afore

dark. Was real sudden. We—we didn't even get off a shot."

The lawman gave that thought. Then, "You any idea who it might've been at Carson City—or maybe your post—that could have had those bushwhackers waiting for you?"

"Nope, sure don't. Word just got out somehow. Told my boys—to keep shut tight—but maybe—maybe the lieutenant let slip—"

"Lieutenant?"

A spasm of coughing shook Exter. When it was over he nodded weakly and said: "Yeh—young fellow. Didn't know him. Started out—him in command. Took sick—was while we was crossing—Utah—or maybe it was still Nevada. Anyways, he turned back."

"Could be he was the leak," the marshal said. "When he left you why didn't you pull into one of the forts that are between there and here for new orders?"

The sergeant's shoulders moved slightly. "What for? Had my orders—part of them was to stay—plumb clear of —of everybody. And I for damn sure didn't need another wet-nosed shavetail to worry over!"

Rye nodded his understanding. Drawing his pistol, he aimed at one of the vultures that had been emboldened by the quiet in the hollow and was swinging in lower. The bullet clipped through the bird's wing feathers, sent it flapping frantically back into the sky.

"Marshal, I'd like to ask a couple of favors," Exter said. His voice was weaker, and words were coming with greater difficulty than moments earlier.

"Do what I can—"

"You here—on lawing business?"

"Yeh. Headed for a town called Crisscross," Rye replied. "Somewhere to the south and east, near as I can remember."

"Recollect seeing the name on my map. I'd be obliged if you'd take my papers and whatever you can find on my men and send it all to the post commander at Fort Union. I'd—I'd appreciate your letting him know what—happened, too."

"Can depend on it," the lawman said. "You know any of that bunch that jumped you, or what they looked like? Maybe you've seen a picture, or a wanted circular or something on one of them—"

"Nope," Exter said slowly, frowning. He was fighting to maintain his faculties. "Was—was like I told you. Happened fast. We was all down, and—and about everybody was dead—'cepting me—right off. Was three, maybe four of them—recollect that."

Exter's mind was drifting, the lawman realized. Earlier the sergeant had said there were a half a dozen outlaws in the party.

"They headed south—with the wagon—"

"You certain about that?" Rye asked, leaning over the soldier to better hear his fading words.

"Yeh—damn sure. South."

This was what fueled the fires of hatred within John Rye for the lawless; six good men doing their duty, sent into a trap and mercilessly slaughtered. The country could never become a decent place for people to live in until all killers, such as these who had taken part in this cold-blooded murder, were brought to justice and made to pay with their lives for their crimes.

"I'll be going in that direction, more or less, myself," Rye said grimly. "I'll be watching for them."

"Hoping you'll catch up," Exter said. "But, but you'll do what I'm asking—let the Army know. These were all—good men—had families—relatives. And that gold—"

"Can rest easy, leave it to me," the marshal said, a kinder note in his voice. Anger was burning bright within him, and a determination to track down the killers, an easy chore since they were moving an iron-tired, heavily loaded wagon, had become foremost in his mind.

"Can leave it to me," Rye said again, and looked more closely at the army sergeant. The man's glazing eyes were on the circling buzzards overhead.

"Sure—like it—if you could do something—about them bastards, too. Hanging up there—just watching and—waiting. Ain't right—man having his bones—picked clean by—"

"I'll see they don't get to you—or any of your men," Rye said, and stopped short.

A wry, down-curving smile had pulled the corners of Henry Exter's mouth into a grimace, and his eyes had taken on a flat haze. He was dead.

The lawman considered the soldier for a long minute. Then, moving nearer, he went through the man's pockets and extracted everything he could find—papers, coins, a bit of folding money, a knife, and what evidently was a good luck charm—and packaged them in Exter's yellow neckerchief.

Rising, he followed a like procedure with the remaining soldiers, noting as he did that all appeared to be middle-aged, seasoned men. Finished with that chore, Rye put the collection of neckerchiefs in his saddlebags and then laid several of the issue blankets, taken from the rolls on the saddles, in the deep wash. Dragging the bodies of the soldiers to the cavity, and adding their weapons, Rye covered them over with the rest of the blankets. With a spade taken also from one of the trooper's saddles, he caved in the side of the ravine and completed the burial.

Sweating profusely, his hatred for the outlaws who had committed the murders becoming more intense with the passage of minutes, Rye mounted his horse and pointed him southward.

He would have liked very much—and was sorely tempted—to ignore the problems that were awaiting him in the town of Crisscross, and concentrate on tracking down the murderous outlaws who had slain Sergeant Henry Exter and his patrol of cavalrymen. But this he could not do; his primary obligation was to the settlement, and it had to be honored.

There was no reason, however, why he could not keep an eye out for the killers en route.

CHAPTER 3

Twice during the remainder of the journey to Crisscross
John Rye encountered the wheel tracks of the stolen army
wagon. They were leading in the same general direction
in which he thought the settlement lay, and it set him to
wondering—and hoping—if the killers' destination might
also be Crisscross.

But as he drew nearer to the town, approaching on the
road coming in from the north, he saw no further signs of
the vehicle's broad prints, and he reckoned the outlaws
were continuing on southward. That assumption stirred a
wave of disappointment and regret within him. It was
certain now that he'd have to forget about the killers,
about the ruthless murders of six men, and the theft of
two hundred thousand dollars in government gold, and
let the Army or some other authority handle the matter.
Deep in his mind he had nurtured the wish that there
might be some connection between the outlaws and the
settlement, and that he would be afforded the opportunity of working on both the murders and the problem facing Crisscross at one and the same time, but such wasn't
proving to be the case—and the town came first.

Shortly before midday Rye reached the lip of the shallow valley in which the settlement was established. The
source of its calling was not difficult to determine; from

the vantage point where he had halted, the lawman could
see the intersection of three different roads a short distance above the collection of structures that made up the
town, all making common use of the log bridge that
spanned a wagon-length-wide stream cutting a fairly
straight course along the settlement's west side.

There appeared to be little activity underway at that
hour, which did not strike the marshal as unusual.
Women usually did their marketing during the early or
late hours when it was cooler, and few persons except
those required by duty chose to move about during the
noonday heat. But as Rye slowly descended the gradual
slope and reached the end of the main street along which
business buildings and a few residences stood, he was
struck by the town's deserted appearance.

Actually, the saloon to his immediate right looked to
have a number of customers, if the horses waiting slack-
hipped and patient at the hitchrack were any indication.
It was designated as the Kansas City by a sign above its
open doorway.

Next in line on the street, the barrenness of which was
relieved somewhat here and there by a cottonwood tree,
was another saloon—the Palo Duro. It was a large, gaud-
ily ornate, prosperous-looking place, and offered to one
and all liquor, women, dancing and the finest gambling
casino west of the Missouri.

Directly opposite it was the Parisian. It had an upper
floor, and with the aid of an oversize likeness of a scantily
clad woman painted on its façade advertised: Clean
Rooms, Beautiful Girls & High Grade Liquor.

The building next to it on that east row was vacant,
and seemingly a favorite target of many high-spirited

marksmen. Windows broken, doors off, plank walls splin-
tered, it was in a sad state of repair, but adjoining it was a
going concern, Nate's Gun & Saddle Shop.

Across from it, as near as Rye could tell from his position at the end of the street, was another abandoned and
badly damaged building. It separated the Palo Duro from
its neighbor, Wolcott's General Store, after which came in
rapid succession more vacant structures—all of which,
even from the distance, showed the effects of considerable hurrahing by overly enthusiastic rowdies in quest
of amusement. Last were the sheriff's office and jail, another empty building, and then a large, sprawling affair of
wood and corrugated tin occupied by Potter's Livery
Stable.

A fourth saloon, the Bonanza, vacant, doors sagging,
glass windows like hollow, sightless eyes, was across from
Wolcott's, and like its counterparts had once marketed
women, whiskey and gambling. But for some reason it
had not survived in a town that clearly concentrated on
fulfilling the pleasure requirements of men in the area.

The only other business house in Crisscross that seemed
to be operating was the Bluebird Restaurant, which, except for more vacant store buildings and residences, was
the final structure on that side of the street.

There was still no one in sight along the broad, ravaged
lane—not even on the porches and landings fronting the
concerns that were alive and open for business; nor had
he seen anyone around the houses lying at the edge of
town that had been visible to him as he rode in. The
church, he noted, a small, narrow affair with a steeple and
a bell, had been boarded up, and the schoolhouse, also of
limited dimension, was likewise closed.

A heavy silence hung over the town; there were no sounds of men at work, of women going about their household chores, of children at play, or of dogs barking. There was nothing that a man would expect to hear in a place where people lived.

Rye, features grim, considered it all thoughtfully. It was as if the town had been closed to all but a select few merchants, and no one else was permitted to do business or live within its limits. He had understood the problem in Crisscross was a need for a lawman; he was beginning to think now that matters ran much deeper than that.

He wondered how long the town had been without a sheriff. He'd not been told when it was that Charley Gaskol had been found murdered in the ragged brakes country east of the settlement, only that it had occurred. It would seem the death had been some time ago—a period of time so extensive that the lawless element, with the apparent sanction of the merchants, had taken over. He had been advised of that, but there'd been no mention of the fact that the decent people had been driven out of Crisscross, and the settlement had become a hell-town. A taut grin split John Rye's mouth. Taking over Gaskol's job was going to amount to much more than he'd figured.

Raking the chestnut lightly with his spurs, the lawman moved on. He drew abreast of the Kansas City, his horses walking slow, plodding wearily, puffs of powder-dry dust shooting up from beneath their hoofs at each step. A sense of wariness began to fill Rye; he realized that he was entering a town in which outlaws would be taking refuge, and many, undoubtedly, would know him.

His passing aroused no one at the Kansas City, and he continued on, casting a glance as he did at the Parisian on his left. Its entrance was empty also, but the pale, oval face of a woman looked down questioningly at him from a second floor window.

And then, abruptly, the carved swinging doors of the Palo Duro flung open. Rye jerked the chestnut to a stop as a squat figure—bearded, hat on the back of his head— plunged out onto the saloon's porch.

"You lousy bastard—I been waiting for my chance to blow your guts out!"

Rye, hand instantly on the butt of his pistol, forefinger seeking the weapon's finely honed trigger, stared at the man coldly.

"Who the hell are you?" he demanded. The squat gun- man stirred no part of his memory.

"Virg Cahoon, that's who I am. Was you that jugged me back in seventy-three!"

Cahoon . . . Rye remembered. Cahoon had killed a man and he had brought him in. The judge had sentenced the outlaw to hang but Cahoon had escaped and quickly lost himself in the broad, disorderly frontier.

"You ain't hauling me in again!" Cahoon yelled, and brought up his arm.

The lawman had noticed the empty holster on the man's hip, which could only mean that he had already drawn his gun, was holding it in his hand, out of sight.

The expected advantage Virg Cahoon had contrived fell short. Rye, rocking slightly to one side on his saddle, drew and fired all in one fluid motion. The bullet slammed into Cahoon's chest, knocked him back a full step before he could get off a shot from the pistol held in his hand. A moment later, as the reflex action of his mus- cles fired the weapon he was convulsively clutching and sent the bullet into the roof of the Palo Duro's porch, he stumbled forward and sprawled full length onto the dusty floor. Only three persons, attracted by the gunshots, appeared in the batwing entrance to the Palo Duro. All men, they paused in the opening briefly, and then came on out onto the porch—mute evidence that the firing of weapons here in Crisscross, as in most frontier towns, attracted only casual interest.

Holstering his weapon, and ignoring the long hitch-rack at the side of the saloon, Rye immediately rode in close. Dismounting, he ground-reined the gelding. Stepping up to Cahoon's body, the lawman claimed the outlaw's dropped pistol and thrust it under his own belt.

"Name's John Rye," he stated in a voice meant to carry. "I'm the new lawman here."

The trio standing on the porch stared. "Rye?" one of them echoed.

Nodding, the marshal again drew his pistol, this time rodding out the spent cartridge and reloading with a fresh one. Again the swinging doors of the Palo Duro opened, and a half a dozen more men, apparently hearing his words, crowded out onto the porch. And to either side, at the Kansas City and Wolcott's store, as well as the occupied buildings on the opposite side of the street, more people were suddenly in evidence.

Rye, finished with his weapon, let it slip back into the holster. Glancing about, he allowed his hard gaze to touch all in sight.

"I reckon this is as good a time as any to do some talking," he said. "Now, I don't know what's happened to this town, but I've got a pretty good hunch, and if what I figure's true, things are going to change mighty quick."

"Who'd you say you was?" a rider—a working cowhand from appearances—asked as he came off the Parisian's porch and started across the street.

"John Rye, special mar—"

"I knowed it—I knowed it—soon as I seen you!" the man shouted, glancing triumphantly about. "You're the one they call the Doomsday Marshal!"

The lawman made no response, neither denying nor admitting the agnomen. A low whistle came from the direction of the Kansas City.

"Him—sure'n hell!" a voice declared. "Seen him once down San Antone way. Busted up some jasper real bad when the fellow tried giving him a hard time. He's a mean one, I'll tell you for sure."

Rye wheeled slowly, faced the speaker. It was another cowhand, in town for a good time apparently.

"I don't know you, friend," the lawman said quietly, "but seems you know me."

"Like I said, I seen you down—"

"That man you're talking about was probably breaking the law—or had already. Best you and everybody else understands this—when I arrest a man it's up to him whether he comes along peaceable or not."

A well-dressed, dark faced man, a cigar between his teeth, pushed through the still-growing crowd on the Palo Duro's porch. He had the clean, smooth look of a riverboat gambler, and when he halted in front of Rye his lips were parted into a half smile.

"I'm Ben Delano," he said, offering his hand to the lawman. "This place is mine, and I'm here to apologize for the, well, for the welcome you got. Want you to know I had nothing to do with Cahoon trying to cut you down—

he's just another customer. You step inside I'll show you a real welcome. The drinks, my girls, the casino—they're all yours any time you're ready."

Rye accepted the man's hand, found it surprisingly firm. "Obliged, but no thanks. Expect to be a little busy around here for a spell."

"For damn sure—just staying alive," a voice in the crowd commented dryly.

"Lawmen don't last long around here," another voice added. "It plain ain't healthy being one."

"Hell, you ain't going to scare no ring-tailed wonder like him—like this here Doomsday Marshal," a man standing at the end of the porch said. There was a distinct thread of sarcasm in his tone.

Rye flicked the speaker with a narrow glance, a small, thin fellow with close-set eyes and a hooked nose. He couldn't recall him from the past.

"Expect I can manage to stick around as long as I'm told to," the lawman said.

Delano nodded, smiled genially. "Expect you will, all right, Marshal. Just don't listen to old Toby, there. He's just shooting off his mouth. Who'd you say sent you here to take over?"

"Don't remember saying but my orders came from Washington—the capital. Seems the governor of the territory asked for help. They sent me."

"I see. Then you know about the last lawman we had, Sheriff Gaskol. Was found bushwhacked—murdered."

"I've been told."

"Man ahead of him had the same tough luck. Can't recall what happened to the one before him." Delano studied the tip of his cigar thoughtfully. "I think he just rode out one day and never come back."

"Just what he did, Ben," a bystander volunteered. "We never did know where he went."

"Was a smart thing to do, considering," the saloon keeper said. "Just wasn't doing any good at his job here. It's a pity Gaskol didn't do the same—he'd be alive somewhere today."

There was a humorless smile on John Rye's lips. "You trying to tell me something, mister?"

Immediately a hush fell over the gathering on the Palo Duro's porch and in the street fronting it. Delano shrugged.

"Just being friendly, Marshal, that's all."

Rye's mouth tightened. "Obliged, but I'll look after myself."

Raising his eyes, the lawman swept the faces of the men on the porch, drifted on to touch those of the crowd in the street. The gathering had increased now to thirty or perhaps forty persons.

"Want to make something clear," he said, again in a far-reaching voice. "If any of you've got big ambitions like Cahoon, I'm ready and willing to accommodate you. All you need do is speak up."

Rye's words carried the length of the hushed street. When he paused and looked about expectantly, a muttering came from a group near the Kansas City, but no one accepted his challenge.

The same dry smile on his lips, Rye continued, "I'm plenty sure there's a few more of you like Cahoon out there, burning to put lead in me because of something I did to you in the past—so I'll be watching and waiting.

"Meantime, I want to give you all a bit of advice. Any man on the wrong side of the law had best mount up and ride out. I aim to clean up this place—no matter what it takes."

"Now, Marshal, hold on a minute," Ben Delano said hastily. "We—this town—depends on folks like these!"

"What town?" Rye countered scornfully. "From what I can see of it you've driven out all of the decent people and turned it into a hell-hole for the benefit of a bawdy house, a couple of saloons, a gun shop, and two or three other merchants who're probably hand-in-glove in on the deal, too."

"We never drove anybody out," Delano said defensively. "Was their idea—"

"I'd like to hear what they've got to say about it," Rye cut in. "Expect it would be different from what you're telling me."

"They'd be lying," Delano said with an indifferent shrug. "Anyway, you've no right to come in here, interfere with business. We've all got to make a living."

"I've got no quarrel with that, and any decent man's welcome to spend every copper he's got in his pockets in your place or the others. But outlaws, killers, and the like, are through. They're not welcome any more. You've made this place a hide-out for any owl-hoot on the run. That's done with, finished! Any of their kind shows up from here on will have to deal with me—and that goes for the ones roosting here now. That clear to everybody?"

Rye again glanced over the crowd, his probing eyes pale, glittering agates beneath their shelf of brows and partly shaded by the brim of his flat-crowned hat tipped well forward. There were a few murmurs of assent, but on the whole the gathering remained silent.

Reaching up, the lawman brushed at the sweat collected on his forehead and nodded curtly. "Pleased you all understand. There an undertaker still around?"

For several moments there was no reply, and then a man standing near the Palo Duro's doorway said: "Yeh, Potter down at the livery stable. He does the planting nowadays."

"Get him—tell him to take care of Cahoon," Rye said brusquely. "The man's probably got a horse and some gear that'll do to sell and pay whatever costs there might be." Pivoting, the marshal crossed to the chestnut and swung up into the saddle.

"Anybody wants to talk to me, I'll be in the sheriff's office," he said. Throwing a calculating look at the crowd as if assessing the possibility of danger and finding it lacking, he rode on down the street.

CHAPTER 4

Rye, the remainder of his ride down the silent street confirming his impression that Crisscross was deserted except for a favored few, drew to a halt in front of the combination sheriff's office and jail. A gust of anger and impatience swept him. Someone, or perhaps it had been several persons, had shown their contempt for the law by nailing boards over the door, and scrawling upon one: *For Rent.*

Climbing off the chestnut, the marshal crossed to the landing fronting the office. Taking a firm grip on the planks, he ripped them free. Then he threw open the door, noting as he did that the lock had been broken.

The heat, trapped inside the closed building, hit him with solid force when he entered. Crossing to a hallway leading from the office, off of which the cells lay, he made his way to the rear of the jail. A drop bar in iron brackets secured the heavy panel; removing the thick length of oak, Rye placed it in a convenient corner and opened the door. Immediately a fresh if not too cool draft of air began to flow through the structure.

For a few moments the lawman remained framed in the doorway, his anger diminishing slowly as he considered the small house and stable with a nearby water pump and trough behind the jail. Such would be quarters for himself and his horses, he assumed. The arrangement appealed to him; at night he'd not be far from his responsibilities.

Coming about, Rye retraced his steps along the corridor, again taking note of the two cells with their solidly built cots and rumpled blankets, and returned to the office. A thick coat of yellow dust covered everything, and that brought to mind again the question of how long the town had been without a lawman; for a lengthy bit of time, it would seem.

There were no rifles or shotguns in the wall rack, he saw, and reckoned the ones that had been there, loaded and ready for use, had been stolen. Hanging Cahoon's pistol by the trigger guard on one of the nearby pegs, the marshal turned to the desk and absently drew out the top drawer. A disarray of papers, among which he noted the key to the cells, and an official-looking document certifying that one Aaron Burke had been sworn in as a deputy, all but filled it.

He tried the other compartments, found them empty, stripped of even the usual stack of outlaw wanted posters that were common in every lawman's office in the country. Someone interested in protecting himself and others had evidently taken pains to remove them.

At a sound in the rear of the jail, Rye stepped back against the wall. Arms folded across his chest, he waited. There was the hard strike of boot heels on the bare floor of the hall, and then a man somewhere in his late fifties stepped into view. Of average height, beardless but with a full mustache, dressed in ordinary work clothing—gray shirt, vest, denim pants, worn boots—and wearing an old army hat, he was pinning a deputy sheriff's star on the pocket of the shirt as he entered. This would be Aaron Burke, the lawman surmised.

Halting, the man fixed small, sharp eyes on Rye, nodded, and coming forward, extended his hand.

"Howdy, Marshal. Name's Burke. I am—or maybe I best say I was—Charley Gaskol's deputy."

Rye took Burke's fingers into his own. "Deputy," he repeated in a cool voice. "You ashamed to be seen wearing that star?"

"No, sir, not ashamed—just too smart," Burke replied frankly. "Ain't good for your health around here to be a lawman."

Rye continued to study the man, not certain that he trusted or even liked him. Judgment would be reserved until later.

"Way I heard it, and from what I've seen, this town's needing a lawman. Surprises me some to find one here not doing anything about the problem."

Aaron Burke's thin shoulders stirred. "Can see how you'd feel that way, Marshal, and I ain't proud of how I've been acting. Expect if I'd a'gone ahead and done the way Charley was doing, they'd a'found me out there in the brakes like they did him—deader than a doornail— and we wouldn't be standing here right now talking."

"No, guess we wouldn't—"

"Just seemed to make more sense to me to stay alive and wait till a new man come along and took over the sheriffing job, and do what I could to help him. Ain't no one man can stand up against what's going on here in Crisscross."

John Rye gave that thought. There was good sense in the deputy's attitude—at least it was logic of the safe kind. He was not sure that all lawmen in a similar situation would view the matter in that light, though.

"You've pinned your star back on, I see."

Burke nodded. "Yes, sir, I sure have. Seen what happened up there at the Palo Duro and heard what you had to say. Figured I'd start being a deputy again."

Rye's smile was dry. "Won't be a safer job now than before."

"Maybe not, but leastwise we got a genuine lawman now, and I'm sure willing to help out when it comes to cleaning up this town. What you said—that about you're aiming to stay till the government sends in a new man—that how it'll be?"

Rye said, "You can bank on it. How long've things been like this?"

"About a month—that's when Charley got killed—a little more'n a month ago. The law's been having a bad time of it, however, for nigh onto two years. That's about when things started going to hell."

"Want to explain that a bit?" the lawman suggested, moving away from the wall toward the door where there was a slight breeze.

"Sure. That was when Reno and Delano and the others took it in their heads to turn Crisscross into a wide open town."

"The others—who are they?" The answer was evident but he wanted to be certain he had his facts straight.

"Well, like I've done said, there's Delano. You met him. Runs the Palo Duro Saloon. Reno's at the Kansas City. Then there's Vic Lefore, a Frenchman from New Orleans. His place is the Parisian.

"Nate Stout's the man that runs the gun and saddle

shop. Frank Wolcott's got the general store. Then there's
Potter—Jeremiah Potter—at the livery stable. Does a few
other things on the side. Last one in it's Mueller. Owns
the restaurant, the Bluebird. Some call him Dutch or the
Dutchman. Real name's Herman. That makes seven of
them. They just took over the town—had plenty of help
from a couple of gun sharps that work for them, Will
Grissom and Jack Turner—and ever since they run things
to suit themselves, and that means wide open and anything goes."

"Nobody bucked them?"

"Was a few tried, but Grissom and Turner, along with
a few of the hardcases, put a stop to it. I reckon you seen
all of the empty buildings around town. Merchants that
was in them just got froze out, I guess you could say,
along with the decent folk that used to live here. Ain't
hardly nobody here now 'cepting homesteaders and little
ranchers that've got their places off a ways."

"Then the way it works out now, Delano and the
others you named get all the business that comes here?"

"Yes, sir, all of it 'cause they ain't got no competition.
Truth is, the town's here and being run for the benefit of
cowhands and outlaws and whoever else is looking for a
good time. Expect you got the idea of that being the way
of it when you seen how the town had been hurrahed—
signs all shot up, windows busted out, hitching posts
dragged down, buildings going to pieces. Can't fault people for pulling out—them that tried to stay, I mean. That
wild bunch out in the street shooting—wasn't nobody
safe, except them inside the saloons."

"Expect the deal's paying off for Delano and the
others."

"Call themselves the Town Council—you can bet your bottom dollar it is! Hell, they're making a fortune, leastwise them in the saloon business are, and I reckon the rest are doing all right, too. There ain't no pilgrims going through, and there's only one stage a week now, but the cowhands, drovers, hide-hunters, outlaws and such that come in more'n make up for the folks that left or don't come in to buy no more."

"What about Gaskol?"

"Charley started cracking down on the outlaws finally," Burke said, seating himself on one of the benches placed along the wall, "and he got plenty rough on the cowhands that tried tearing up the place, but he never got nowheres doing it."

"He try locking a few of them up?"

"Sure, a couple of times, but it weren't no use. Last time he done it, Delano and a couple other council members showed up, like they'd done before, and ordered Charley to turn his prisoner loose. Heard them tell him plain that this here was their town, and that he'd best forget that star he was wearing.

"They couldn't make Charley unlock the cell, so Grissom got the key and done it. The sheriff told them then and there he aimed to go right on jailing anybody that started trouble—only after that he was going to hide the key. I ain't never known what got Charley riled up and acting like a tough lawman, but I do know that the next day he was found out there in the brakes, a bullet hole in his head."

Rye gave that thought. "Whatever," he said after a time, "Charley Gaskol was a good man. What about the lawmen who were in charge here ahead of him?"

"Was two that took the job after the council started running things their way. Man here just before Charley—I weren't no deputy then—ended up just like him, dead out there in the brakes. Other'n ahead of him climbed on his horse one day and rode off without a good-by, go-to-hell or nothing to anybody."

"Any idea who it was that killed Gaskol?"

Burke brushed away the beads of sweat on his forehead with a faded red bandanna. "Could've been any one of them hardcases hanging around town," he said, "but was I laying odds, I'd bet on it being Will Grissom or Jack Turner—maybe both."

"You've got no doubts the merchants had it done?"

"Not any—and that's for damn sure, just like they've prob'ly got their heads together right now fixing to have you bushwhacked!"

Rye smiled bleakly, shrugged. "Goes with the job," he said, and turned to the window in the north wall of the office. The glass in it, unlike that facing the street, was still intact.

"The other folks—businessmen—living here when it all started, didn't they put up a fight? The kind of people that've got the sand to settle a town like this, go into business and make a home for themselves usually don't scare off easy."

"Didn't—not at first. Them that did have a store tried to stick it out, but the council fixed it so's nobody'd buy off them, and just plain shut them off. And the folks that had been trading with them found out that it was mighty risky buying from anybody but Wolcott and Nate Stout and the rest of the council. About then, I reckon it was, that the hurrahing started. Went on day and night—

yahoos riding up and down the street shooting out windows, filling signs full of holes and dragging down fences and hitching posts.

"Was plain that Delano and his bunch was out to drive everybody—the other merchants and the folks that lived here, too—out of town. And that's just what they done. Some of them I talked to said it wasn't worth chancing their families getting hurt, and I sure can't fault them. Better to go start over somewheres else, flat busted maybe, than let somebody in your family get killed."

Rye stared off past the vacant building adjoining the sheriff's office, to the empty street. The heat was becoming more intense, and small dust devils springing to life here and there raced down the canyon-like area between the structures to disappear suddenly in a yellow haze.

"I would think some of them would've put up a holler—ask for help from the U.S. marshal," Rye said, after a time.

"Somebody did—never knew who," Aaron Burke replied. "Was a deputy come down not long after they found Cartwright—he was the sheriff right ahead of Gaskol—laying out there dead. Hung around for a few days, but naturally Delano and them didn't let him find out nothing. About all he got done was cause a lot of the hardcases to take out for No Man's Land real fast."

John Rye smiled faintly. That strip of lawless land was much too handy to Crisscross. Now that he had shown his face on the street, he guessed he could expect the outlaws with prices on their heads, such as Virg Cahoon, to ride out or at least lie low until he had moved on. It was not that Rye considered himself so formidable, it was simply that men of Cahoon's stripe usually chose to avoid a confrontation; in Virg's case he had simply encountered the outlaw unexpectedly, and the shoot-out was thus forced.

"Don't mean to be putting you down none, Marshal, but I ain't sure one man can do something about the way it is around here. Delano and his friends've got this town whipped around to where it's just the way they want it, and they ain't about to let somebody change things."

"Maybe," Rye murmured absently.

"Now, I know who you are, that you get a pile of respect from everybody, but respect sure ain't going to stop no bullets, and that's what'll be waiting for you soon as they find out they can't scare you off. I reckon you can see that."

Rye nodded. "It's what I expect—but it doesn't change anything. I know what I'm up against now, and like you've said, a reputation won't stop a bullet. But sometimes it does keep one from being fired. Anyway, the law can't ever afford to run. Once that starts, the owl-hoots will take over the country."

Aaron, his eyes bright, brushed at his drooping mustache. The shine of sweat was on his leathery skin, and beads had again gathered on his forehead.

"Figured you'd be talking that way. Charley felt the same only he just wasn't smart. I reckon you are else you wouldn't've got as old as you are—considering the business you're in."

"Not so smart that I think I won't need a good man siding me."

Burke looked down, swallowed hard. "Well, maybe you don't figure me for much, but if you want—"

The marshal's attention was on a dozen or so men

emerging from the Palo Duro and advancing toward the jail. He heard nothing of what the deputy had said.

"Looks like a delegation coming," he murmured.

At once Burke rose and crossed to the window. He swore softly. "It's them," he said, "the whole blasted bunch. Expect they're coming to give you a warning, tell you it'll be best if you move on."

"It's a hot day to be wasting words," Rye said dryly, and added: "I know Delano, mind naming off the others for me?"

Grinning, the deputy moved closer to Rye. "That jasper next to Ben Delano is Vic Lefore," he said. "Likes to wear them fancy duds."

Lefore was a slim, short, dark-skinned man in a suit, white shirt and string tie. Besides a thin line mustache, he also sported a goatee.

"The husky one there that looks like a cowhand and's wearing a pistol—that's Phil Reno."

"Runs the Kansas City."

"Yeh. Somebody said he don't own it, just running it for some fellow back east."

Reno, in cord pants tucked into mid-high boots, red shirt and leather vest did look to be more a hardcase ranch hand than the operator of a saloon.

"Can he handle that iron he's packing or is it just for show?"

"Ain't never seen him use it so I don't know. It's not a new six-shooter, I recollect that, so if a man can go by that, then he's used it a'plenty."

"Unless he got it from somebody who did," the lawman said, eyes fixed on the oncoming group.

The number of persons in the party exceeded by at

least a dozen the seven who made up Crisscross' so-called council, Rye noted. The surplus would be the admiring and the curious, anxious to hear and see the new town lawman put in his place.

"Who's the tall jasper in the dark suit? Looks like he's carrying a grudge against everybody."

Somewhere in his forties, the man had dark, deep-set eyes, and his square-cut face, devoid of both beard and mustache, was set to stern, humorless lines.

"That's Frank Wolcott."

"Not a friendly looking man."

"He ain't. Lost his wife a couple of years ago, and it soured him a'plenty. Man walking beside him—the one wearing spectacles and pants that're a mite big for him— that's Nate Stout. Something's been chawing on him lately, seems sort've worried like. Getting along with Delano and them ain't no cinch, I expect. That's Potter behind him."

Jeremiah Potter, except for Reno, was probably the youngest member of the council. Somewhat stocky, round-faced, with a mustache but no beard, he was wearing bib overalls, no shirt, and heavy boots. A cud of tobacco bulged his left cheek.

"Potter's a pretty good old boy—ain't much like them others," the deputy said. "I think I told you he owns the livery stable. Got a barbershop in one corner of it. Can get a bath there, too."

"He a barber?"

"No, has a fellow that does barbering, name of Joe Gillespie. Joe had a shop of his own here once, other side of the Bonanza. A bunch of drunks busted it up one night, and he just give up—quit. Potter got him to bring his chair and stuff, do his business in a corner of the livery stable."

"Still makes him a part of the council."

"I reckon it does—more or less. They plain don't want any outsiders doing business here, and so far they've kept it that way. Got themselves a hands-down deal. That big, red-faced fellow, that's Dutch Mueller."

"Runs the Bluebird Restaurant, I think you said."

"Yeh. He's a pretty good old boy, too, and I don't think him—or his wife—much likes things the way they are. They just got caught up in it, being the only eating place in town, and had to go along with Delano and the others."

"Could stand up and tell them he wanted out of it."

"Sure—and lose everything he's got. The council would just take over on their terms, then put somebody they could handle to running the place. Dutch ain't the fighting kind—got a wife and a kind of pretty daughter, Helga, in there with him, and he ain't about to let them get hurt. The girl's real smart—was Doc Peterson's nurse before he up and moved away. She's the closest thing we got to a doctor here now."

"That bunch with them—see anybody special? I don't recognize any of them."

"Them two that are off to one side, the tall one with the brown hat—that's Will Grissom. The redhead with him's Jack Turner. Rest are just some of the crowd that lays around the saloons. You won't spot none of the hardcases. They'll keep out of sight till they know what the score is."

Rye nodded. The delegation had reached the front of

the sheriff's office, were slanting for the door. The lawman glanced at Burke.

"If you're still a bit skittish about wearing that star, now's the time to make it plain. Can turn around and head out the back before any of them see you with it. I won't hold it against you, knowing how things have been."

Burke studied John Rye for a long breath, and then shook his head. "I can't fault you for thinking that, Marshal, but after seeing how you handled that Virg Cahoon, and hearing you talk up to all them others, I'd be proud to keep on wearing it—if it's all right with you."

Rye's features were expressionless. He had been fortunate upon arrival to encounter someone friendly to the law, like Aaron Burke, who knew the situation in Crisscross and could furnish him with facts and details. As for the man being one upon whom he could depend in a critical showdown should one develop—he could only hope.

"Fine with me," the marshal said, shifting his attention to the doorway. "It's going to be right interesting to hear what the council has to say."

CHAPTER 5

Ben Delano was the first to enter the office. He was followed closely by his six partners, all looking firm and determined, with sweat glistening on their faces. The remainder of the party halted in the street, with the exception of Grissom and Turner, who took up a slouching stand on the landing, as if on guard.

Rye gave the gunmen cool appraisal while the council members shuffled noisily about on the board floor getting themselves positioned. Both were well armed, and had the cool, withdrawn look of men who would not hesitate to make use of their weapons if it became necessary. The type was no stranger to the lawman. Hired guns—all too often he'd been compelled to deal with their kind.

Rye, arms folded, leaned back against the wall and faced the visitors. Aaron Burke assumed a similar stance nearby.

"Something on your mind?" Rye asked, getting things underway.

"Plenty," Delano snapped. "First off, we're the ones running this town—own it, in fact—and we've got a few words to say to you. Best I introduce my partners—"

"No need," Rye cut in indifferently. "My deputy's already pointed you out by name and business."

Delano glanced at Burke. "Haven't seen you for quite a

spell—figured you'd pulled out," he said, and then came back to Rye. "I reckon you know the score."

"I do," Rye said flatly, "and it don't set well with me. And before you get started I want to get this said—I'll be making some changes around here."

"The hell," Nate Stout muttered, stirring angrily. "You ain't got no right to—"

"Never mind," Delano, evidently the chosen speaker for the group, broke in. "I expect the marshal's a reasonable man. I'm plenty sure we can talk this out."

"Not much to talk out," Rye said. "I've been sent here to establish the law, and I figure to do it."

Delano's thin mouth tightened. "Best you hear what we've got to say before you set your mind to that!" he said sharply. "We—all of us—have spent a lot of money and time getting things set up here so's we can do a fair business."

"You bet!" Reno added. "We worked like hell to get the word spread around that we had an open town—and we sure ain't going to stand by and let you mess things up for us!"

"We've got our own lawman—Will Grissom—so we don't need no outsider," Wolcott said in his stiff way. "We've made that plain."

"If you mean by having the last two killed and running off the one before them, I guess I'll admit that's pretty plain," the marshal said coldly.

"There's no proof that we had anything to do with any of that." Ben Delano's voice was even, controlled, although anger showed in his eyes.

"Maybe not, but it's proof that this town needs law," Rye replied.

"We got law!" Nate Stout declared. "Only killing we've had in a long time was you shooting down Cahoon."

The lawman's features were quiet. "Anytime a man, especially some two-bit outlaw, draws a gun on me he better be able to trigger it fast—or I'll kill him."

Delano wagged his head. "That was bad, bad for business, and a big mistake on your part."

Rye laughed. "Gunning down a killer who was supposed to hang a long time ago? You don't make much sense."

"Could be, but we didn't come to argue about that," Wolcott said. "We're here to tell you—order you—to get out. We don't want you around!"

Again the marshal laughed, this time in a dry, derisive way. He glanced at Aaron Burke, nodded slightly and brought his attention back to the men facing him from across the desk.

"Better understand this—you've got me whether you want me or not! You and your greed have turned a good town into a hide-out for every outlaw on the run, and a hangout for fancy women and drunks, at the expense of some fine people.

"Now you mark it down on your slate—that's going to change! You can't make this piece of ground into a little country of your own where you're all kings. This is the Territory of New Mexico, and a part of the United States. And by God, you're going to live by the law of the land! Understand?"

There was a long minute's hush, and then Delano spoke. "It's you that needs to understand something, Marshal. We've got too much sunk in what we own—in making this the kind of town we want—"

"Meaning a place where outlaws can run loose, do whatever they please—"

"Outlaws ain't the only kind that come here to spend their money," Vic Lefore said, speaking for the first time. His voice was soft-edged, bore the unmistakable touch of the South. "We get ranchers, cowboys, trail drivers, men from other settlements—even travelers."

"I'll have no quarrel with them as long as they behave themselves. If they get out of line, I'll jug them same as I will any man who breaks the law."

"Your law," Wolcott said acidly.

"The law," Rye countered in a harsh voice. "The kind you'll find in any decent town. And once I get things started I'm hoping all those folks you drove out—"

"Who says we drove anybody out?" Nate Stout demanded angrily.

Rye grinned. "There's a lot of empty buildings and houses around. You saying those people just picked up and moved for no reason?"

"Was their idea—"

"Sure—after the bunch of you hatched up your scheme to take over the town. You made it so damned rough on them they had no choice but to pull out."

"That's not exactly the way it was," Delano said, with a side look at Burke, "no matter what you've been told. Some of them wanted to quit, move on. Why, Wolcott there even bought out the stock of a couple who—"

"At maybe a penny on the dollar?" the lawman cut in, eyes on the general store owner.

Wolcott shrugged. "I don't see what that has to do with our being here, either. Fact is, however, they wanted to sell so I bought. Same goes for Potter and Nate Stout. Even the Dutchman. We all helped."

"Doubt if that's the right word for it," Rye said dryly, "but whatever, the town ended up with one general store, one livery stable, one restaurant and one gun shop—and three saloons that've got things all cut and dried between them: one for the hard drinkers, another for the high-toned trade and a third with a good stock of women. You've baked yourself a big pie and you've cut it into seven pieces—"

"And we figure to keep it that way," Wolcott interrupted. "It's how we want it, and any man who tries to change it—well, there ain't none of us going to be responsible for what happens to him."

"That a threat?" Rye asked coolly, touching each of the merchants as well as Grissom, now standing in the doorway, with narrowed eyes.

"No, I reckon you could say it's a friendly warning," Delano replied, taking up the conversation. "You need to understand this, Marshal, it's not only us who want to keep the town the kind it is. The men trading with us want it, too. They know they can find what they're looking for—good liquor, honest gambling, pretty women—and have themselves a big time without a bunch of holy-joes yelling their heads off about it. Hell, we're not the only town in the country that's wide open!"

"But we're the best!" Stout said proudly. "We're getting more new customers all the time!"

"I can believe it," Rye said with a shrug. "A Ranger told me a while back that there's better'n eight thousand outlaws in Texas alone. You'll have most of them over here once they get wind of how easy it is to get by with anything, including murder."

"That'll be our lookout," Lefore said, dismissing the comment. "We can deal with them. We don't need your help."

"And we'd sure hate for our town to be the place where the Doomsday Marshal runs smack into a doomsday bullet," Frank Wolcott added slyly.

"I'm paid to take my chances on that happening," the lawman said. "Now, this yakking's gone on long enough, but before you go I'm advising you to pass the word along that Crisscross is no longer a stopping place or a hide-out for owl-hoots, and that the law is taking over."

"If we do that," Wolcott warned, "all hell's going to bust loose! We won't be responsible for what's liable to happen to you and the deputy."

"We'll take our chances," Rye said.

Reno laughed. "Chances—I reckon that's the right word for it."

Ben Delano raised a hand for silence. "Let's remember that the marshal has a job to do, and try to understand his side of this," the saloon keeper said reasonably. "We're asking him to understand ours, so let's just let the matter ride for a bit, give him—and us—time to think it over."

Rye's eyes were narrowed as he studied the Palo Duro's owner. The man had done an about-face, was now presenting a different attitude, all of which raised the lawman's suspicions.

"Now, that's a right good idea," Jeremiah Potter said, speaking out finally. "Man smart as the marshal ought to see—"

"Nothing to see," Rye cut in curtly. "The law is the

law, and that's how it's going to be around here. I'll be obliged if you'll be on your way. The deputy and I've got work to do."

Wolcott swore deeply, pivoted angrily on a heel and started for the door. Dutch Mueller, round, red face shining with sweat, still silent, followed immediately, as if relieved the meeting was finished. The other members of the council turned also, but halfway across the room Delano paused and looked back over a shoulder.

"Still believe you ought to think this over, Marshal—could mean a lot to you." Before Rye could answer, he stepped out into the bright sunlight and joined his waiting friends.

For a long minute the air of tension that had filled the small, heat-laden office held, and then Rye, smiling, turned to Burke.

"That takes care of that. Now, first off, I'd like to get this place cleaned up. Do you know somebody who—"

"Widow woman out near my place does housework," Burke said before the lawman could finish his question. "I'll get her down here."

The marshal nodded crisply, crossed to the broken window. "Want to get a new glass for this, too."

"I'll take care of it."

Rye nodded, his hooded eyes on the merchants walking slowly down the street. Phil Reno, talking hard, was holding the other men's attention, and once Delano came half about and threw a glance back at the jail.

"No need. Be glad to pay a carpenter or a handy man to do it—and whatever else needs fixing."

"Ain't nobody left around here that can do it, far as I know," the deputy said. "Everybody's moved away 'cepting barflies, cowhands, the gamblers and gunslingers and such, and they sure ain't none of them going to hire out for work like that. Ain't no big to-do, anyway. I'll get the window from Wolcott, put it in myself in no more than ten or fifteen minutes."

"Wolcott—hate having to buy anything from him."

"Well, we have to unless you want to ride to Willow Creek—about fifty miles on west of here."

Rye's shoulders stirred. "That bunch have sure got it worked out good for themselves. Anything you buy in Crisscross comes from one of them."

Burke swore, mopped at the sweat on his face and neck. "That Wolcott sure riles me some! Makes you feel when you do buy something from him that he's doing you a big favor to sell it to you. He's got about as ornery and mean as a fellow can get."

"Kind of like my enemies that way," the marshal said. "Know where they stand. It's the ones talking nice to your face that'll fool you. They're the kind that'll probably stick a knife in your belly while they're shaking your hand."

The council were all turning into the Palo Duro. Rye, wheeling, came back to the desk. Burke had settled again on one of the benches. Legs extended before him, big, worn hands clasped in his lap, he was sitting with shoulders against the wall.

"I want you to realize what you're letting yourself in for if you keep on wearing that star," Rye said. "You can figure on it getting mighty rough around here."

The deputy shrugged. "Beats setting around rusticating," he said, and then, frowning, added: "Hell, Marshal, I know that. I didn't just come in on a load of hay! I ain't much a'scared, but I sure am sick to death of that council bunch and what they've done to this town, my town I reckon I can say, 'cause I've lived here quite a spell. If you're out to change things, then I'm standing with you."

"Good to hear that. What I aim to do is get things headed back the other direction so the new sheriff won't have such a hell of a job to do when he gets here."

"If he gets here," Burke said cynically, smoothing his mustache. "There ain't nobody wants the job."

"Up to me—us—to change that kind of thinking," Rye said. Then, through the open doorway, he caught sight of several vultures circling above something at the edge of town. A change of thought came to his mind, and he asked: "You happen to see an army wagon pass by here early this morning? Or it could've been last night sometime. Likely had four or five riders with it."

The deputy frowned, finally shook his head. "Nope, I sure don't recollect it. Why? It got something to do with your coming here?"

Rye said, "No, there was an ambush," and recounted the details of the incident as he knew them, concluding his words with the information that the outlaws had headed more or less in a southerly direction.

When he had finished, Aaron Burke swore feelingly. "That's mighty bad—pure murder for sure. I can see why it riled you up so."

"What riles me even more is that I can't do anything about it," the lawman said. "It would've been easy to follow those wheel tracks, but I figured I had to come on here where I'd been sent, and let somebody else take care of it. When's the next stage going south pass through?"

Burke thought briefly. "I reckon it'll be tomorrow."

"Good. I've got the belongings of those soldiers I want to send to Fort Union, along with a report of what happened."

"Well, if that bunch keeps going south like they started, they'll end up at the fort, and that'll make it easy for the provost marshal. He can be waiting for them. You want to take a look at your house? It's right out back."

"Might as well," Rye said. Coming out from behind the desk, he followed the deputy down the narrow corridor out to the rear of the building where the cottage stood. Entering, the marshal found it small, sparsely furnished and like his office covered by a thick layer of dust.

"Can have the woman clean up here, too," Burke said. "And if you're wanting I'll get you some grub while I'm at Wolcott's so's you'll have something on hand."

"Little tired of my own cooking," the lawman said, "so I'll do my eating at the Bluebird. And I don't want anybody getting the idea that I'm skittish about being seen on the street. That stable I saw good enough to keep my horses in?"

"Yeh. Don't think the roof leaks, and the sides'll hold out the wind, but you can put your animals in Potter's place."

"As soon keep them close where they'll be handy."

"Prob'ly a smart thing to do," the deputy agreed. "I'll see to some hay and grain, and fill up the water trough."

Rye considered the older man with a slight frown. "Appreciate all this you're doing for me, Aaron, but just because you're the sheriff's deputy don't mean you have to do hired-hand work, too."

"Maybe not," Burke said, starting for the door and the two horses at the hitchrack in front of the jail, "but I've been hoping and wishing for a man like you to come along and take over, and I'm sure going to do everything I can to help you get the job done. You want your gear in here or in the office?"

"Saddlebags in there, rest of it in here'll be fine," Rye said, and moved for the doorway also. "Think I'll have me a look around town while you're getting things squared away."

CHAPTER 6

Ben Delano, listening idly to Phil Reno's steady monotone as he lamented the bad luck they had encountered in the shape of Marshal John Rye, looked back over his shoulder as, with the others, he walked toward his business.

"I been hearing all these years about lawmen getting paid to look the other way, but damn it all, I ain't never run into one. All them I've run into've been so pure and honest they stunk!"

"Only thing we can do is take care of him same way we did Gaskol," Wolcott said.

"I ain't sure it'll be all that easy where this bird's concerned," Potter commented. "I've heard about him. He ain't no come-every-day lawman."

"Guess that's how he got that handle—Doomsday Marshal," Stout said. "Ain't nobody yet ever got the best of him, they say, and he always gets the job done that he's sent out to do."

"Which backs up what I just said," Wolcott pointed out. "We've got to get shut of him, fast."

"Way I see it, too," Vic Lefore agreed. "And the sooner we get rid of that bastard, the better for us. What do you say, Nate?"

Ben Delano glanced back again, this time to see if any of the hangers-on who had followed them to the sheriff's office was in earshot. The majority of the crowd, finding the heat much more oppressive than the meeting was interesting, had gone on to seek out the cooler comfort of their favorite saloon. Only Grissom and Jack Turner were still with the party, and both of them, having been hired before to perform confidential tasks, were trustworthy.

"I'll string along with you fellows," Stout replied, mopping at the sweat on his face. "You know that."

"Dutch, how about you?" Lefore asked, centering his attention on the restaurant man.

Mueller's round face had taken on an even deeper red from the driving heat, and moisture stood out on his forehead in large beads. He slid a look at his place of business, noted both his wife, Gerta, and daughter, Helga, at the window watching him and the other members of the council pass by.

"Murder I do not like," he said haltingly, "and there is something about this man Rye that is a warning, but it is a matter I will leave up to you."

"That mean you'll go along with whatever we decide to do—just like always?" Reno pressed.

"Yah, just like before," Mueller answered in his thickly accented voice.

"Then I reckon we got it all settled," Lefore said, with a direct look at Grissom. "When do you figure—"

"Let's slow this down a bit," Delano cut in, making known his thoughts. "Could be we won't have to go that far, and I'm hoping we don't. This Rye's a big, important man in the law enforcement business, and if something happens to him like happened to Gaskol and Cartwright, we could find a half a dozen U.S. marshals, and maybe the U. S. Army coming down on us."

Wolcott halted, an angry frown on his features as he confronted the saloon man. "Then what do you say we ought to do? Holding off could be a big mistake, too. You got some plan up your sleeve?"

Delano nodded. "A couple, in fact. I'd like to let Mada work on him some. Straight as this Rye is, he's still a man —and human."

Reno hawked, spat into the dust. "Well, I'll say this, if anybody can bust him down it'll be Mada. What else you got in your head? You said a couple of things."

Ben Delano raised his gaze, looked ahead. The swinging doors of the Palo Duro were near. It would be good to get inside out of the sun, and have a drink. A half smile parted his thin lips.

"I've yet to meet a man who didn't have a price, if the offer was big enough," he said, confidentially. "Come on in—I'll set up the drinks and we can finish talking."

CHAPTER 7

As Aaron Burke crossed to the hitchrack, jerked loose the chestnut's reins and turned to lead the big gelding and the gray pack horse to the stable behind the jail, John Rye moved off down the street.

There were now no signs of the Crisscross merchants, all having entered the Palo Duro where they apparently were gathering and holding a further discussion of the situation that faced them. Rye's mouth pulled into a taut grin as he strode slowly along the broad, dusty street in the strong sunlight. He reckoned that for damn sure he'd upset their applecart, and it wasn't difficult to imagine how they felt about him. That they would take measures to maintain things in the settlement as they were was a certainty. The fact that they had gotten rid not only of Charley Gaskol, but the two lawmen who had preceded him as well, was proof of that.

The smile on the marshal's lips tightened as the thought brought to mind his own need to be wary. From this moment on he'd best keep his eyes open for dark shapes in the shadows, for furtive movements at a window or doorway of one of the vacant buildings. And he should be on the alert for and suspicious of being drawn out of town for some reason—particularly in the direction of the brushy, broken brakes country to the east where they had found the lifeless bodies of Charley Gaskol and the sheriff who had served ahead of him.

The council would find plenty of volunteers for the job of cutting him down if Virg Cahoon was a fair sample of the outlaws hanging around town. But John Rye reckoned that would be true no matter where he went; there would always be somebody somewhere looking for the chance to put a bullet in his head.

The lawman's step slowed. Eyes switching from side to side as he trod the deserted street in the mid-afternoon heat, he had seen the dual trail of wagon wheels on the green slope of a hill a short distance west of the settlement. In all probability the paralleling prints would have escaped his notice had they been narrower, and the grass caught within them not so completely crushed. But with the green blades pressed tight to the ground, indicating the passage of wide tread, iron-tired wheels bearing a considerable load, the tracks reflected the sun's rays much as did water.

Veering from course, Rye turned left off the street and followed a path running alongside the empty building standing adjacent to Wolcott's General Store. Angling then to the creek which lay on beyond, he made use of a two-log footbridge and crossed to the hillside where he had spotted the tracks. Tension began to build within him as he squatted beside the prints and made a closer examination.

Unquestionably they were the tracks of the type wheels used on army wagons—and they weren't too old. Rye could see where the bent blades of grass were beginning to lift themselves and stand erect again. Could this be the vehicle the slain soldiers had been escorting, or was it merely one belonging to some passing pilgrim or local resident?

Rye mulled that about in his mind as he came to his feet. There was a good possibility the wagon was the stolen army vehicle, but chances were equally strong that it had belonged to a party of migrants passing through. The lawman doubted it was the property of some local resident; according to Aaron Burke there were few families still living in the area.

Raising his gaze, Rye traced the tracks as far as they were visible to him. They appeared to have come out of the northwest, circled the hill and continued northeast—or it could be the exact opposite. The importance of the answer to that was immediately clear to Rye.

Nothing was to be gained by pursuing the prints westward, he decided, since it would take him away from town, but if he followed their course into the northeast, which paralleled the settlement, he just might determine whether the wagon had been coming or going when it passed by.

Glancing about and carefully noting the rear of the buildings in the distance, the lawman began to make his way alongside the deeply pressed prints. Shortly a fact became apparent to him: in a small stretch of loose sand where a ravine had provided a bed for infrequent rain water, the tracks, small and distinct as if made by mules, showed plainly the wagon had come from the west.

Rye's suspicions mounted steadily to conviction. A heavy wagon drawn by mules—the usual army system, and it could have come from the direction the dying sergeant, Henry Exter, had said it had headed. Assuming that Crisscross had been the teamster's destination, tem-

porarily or otherwise, he probably had overshot the settlement, or was forced by the hill's bulk to circle and double
back, keeping a safe distance from the town nevertheless.
But where were the rest of the men who had been in on
the ambush? There were no signs of riders accompanying
the vehicle.

There could be good reason for such, Rye concluded
after puzzling over it. The riders could have left the
wagon earlier, sending it on across country alone so that
it would attract no attention. And there could be other
reasons for their absence, all of which were relatively
unimportant at the moment; what was important was to
stay with the wagon tracks and see where they led to.

Rye resumed his trailing of the prints. They still followed no established road or trail, simply cut across open
ground, winding in and out of waist-high brush at times,
angling over grassy slopes now and then. Again the lawman glanced to his right. He was now well opposite the
north end of the town, a good quarter mile from the end
building on that west side of the street—Phil Reno's Kansas City Saloon.

Rye slowed, brushed at the sweat on his face as a jack
rabbit spurted suddenly from a clump of sage nearby and
raced off in periodic high bounds. The lawman wished
now he had taken his horse; he hadn't expected to do so
much walking. But it was too late to think about that
now. Resting for a minute or so, he continued, soon
finding the going a bit easier when the tracks began to
descend a slight grade. He seemed to be pointing for the
creek, Rye realized; it was angling more to the west in
this area.

Abruptly Rye came to a halt. A shallow valley through

which the stream flowed fell away from the plain across which he had been moving. In its center stood a small house, a homesteader from appearances, and one clearly deserted. Close by was a barn with a fenced-in yard—an enclosure too small to be termed a corral, but that was of no significance; what was were the four mules standing hipshot within it.

Rye dropped to a crouch and for several minutes studied the homestead, searching for signs of life other than the mules. Seeing none, he moved swiftly down the grade toward the house, keeping to the brush as much as possible. Sweat clothing him, the marshal gained the forward corner of the aging structure and stopped. From where he now stood he had a clear look at the mules. All bore the army brand, a bold U.S. Satisfaction rolled through the lawman; his suspicions had been justified.

But to what end? A prod of conscience sent that question into John Rye's mind. He was there to establish law and order in the town of Crisscross, not spend his time on a matter that should be left to parties more directly concerned, such as the Army at Fort Union or the U. S. Marshal's office in Santa Fe.

That was all true and he readily recognized the fact, but as a lawman he could hardly turn his back on a situation involving massacre and theft when it presented itself to him. No good lawman could, he assured himself, and swung his attention back to the mules.

If these were the animals that had drawn the wagon transporting the gold—and there was no doubt in Rye's mind that they were—where was the vehicle? And where were the horses the outlaws rode? Logically, they should

be in the barnyard with the mules. And the outlaws—
where were they?

He'd best start with the house, the marshal decided. It
could be some, or all, of the killers were inside resting, or
perhaps sleeping. Quietly, Rye made his way along the
wall of the house to a partly open door. Reaching it, he
listened intently for a time. There were no sounds, and
drawing his pistol, he quickly entered.

He could find no one, only indications that the dusty,
empty rooms had been used occasionally by drifters in
need of a place to spend a night. Holstering his weapon,
the lawman returned to the yard. Still cautious, he
headed for the barn that stood to the left of the yard.

The mules looked up hopefully as he passed, apparently in need of feed and water despite the open gate
through which they could depart and forage on their
own. He'd see to their needs before he left, Rye thought,
and walked quietly on to the open doorway of the larger
building.

A half a dozen strides short of the entrance Rye drew
to a stop. The wheel tracks of the wagon on the baked
ground before him were dimly evident. Stepping to one
side to avoid framing himself in the wide opening,
thereby eliminating the possibility of being seen by someone inside the structure, Rye again brought out his pistol,
and eased in close to the doorway.

Again there was only the buzz of insects and the rest-
less stamping of the mules to be heard. Hunched low,
Rye hurriedly stepped into the barn and flattened himself
in the deep shadows along the near wall. No blast of
weapons, not even a shout had challenged him; the barn

was deserted, as was the house. But standing in the center of the littered, dirt floor was the army wagon.

What had taken place was apparent. The killers had driven the vehicle to the old, abandoned homestead—an indication that they knew of it in advance—and there in privacy relieved it of the gold it carried.

Moving in close to the wagon, Rye saw the boxes of supplies the vehicle was transporting as a blind for its true mission cast to one side. The planks in the center area of the wagon bed had been pried up to reveal the compartment in which the chest of gold coins had been secreted.

Removing it, and likely dividing the gold eagles among themselves at the time, the outlaws had then ridden on, heading for a distant point such as Dodge City where they could enjoy their riches. Or, if they were some of the hardcases that hung around Crisscross, they could have slipped back into town.

Regardless, the outlaws, whoever they were, would be too smart to spend any of the new gold for some time to come. But there was always a chance one of them would make a mistake and—

A gunshot coming from the town brought the lawman's speculations to an abrupt halt, and brought to mind again his true purpose for being there. At once he pivoted, and leaving the barn, started for town at a run. He'd return later and have a closer look at the wagon, see if he could turn up something that would tell him who the outlaws that had brought it there might be.

CHAPTER 8

Entering the Palo Duro, Ben Delano led his associates through the slim, afternoon crowd to a large, circular table in a back corner of the saloon.

He was proud of his establishment, and took pains to keep his gamblers on the square, the few women who were there clean and his whiskey honest and unwatered. Delano believed there was plenty of money to be made from a clientele who appreciated the finer aspects, and he was perfectly willing to let the Parisian and the Kansas City split what was left over.

As the other men drew back chairs and prepared to settle down, Delano signaled Al Glenn, one of the bartenders, for a bottle and glasses. Drawing a cigar from his pocket, he sat down also.

"Appears to me that sonofabitch's hurting business already," Nate Stout commented, glancing around. "Sure ain't much of a crowd in here."

"Usually light this time of day," Delano replied. "Can tell more about it tonight."

"My hunch is it'll be the same story," Wolcott said, leaning back. "I'm for getting rid of him fast."

Delano waited until Glenn had set a bottle of the best Bourbon and a clutch of glasses on the table. Then, as the bartender moved off, he said, "We don't want to make a mistake—like getting the Army sent here and putting us under martial law."

"Amen to that," Jeremiah Potter said. "I remember once when a bunch of hardcases took over a town where I was working, and the government sent in a whole company of soldiers. Was a major in command, a real bluenose, and he straightened that town out in a hurry. We sure don't want none of that here."

"It's not likely to happen," Vic Lefore said, fingers encircling his glass as Delano filled it. "I think you're all forgetting something—there's nobody living in this town any more but us, and the people working for us, so who's going to complain to the government? Ain't none of us about to."

"Somebody sure did. Look how quick they sent Rye in here when Gaskol turned up dead," Potter remarked.

"Was the same with Cartwright," Wolcott recalled. "There's a few people still living out in the county. Expect it was one of them."

Reno shook his head. "Just give me a couple more years of us owning the town like we do, and they can have it! I'll have me a stake big enough by then to pack up and move on, find myself a good place to light and take it easy."

There was silence after that, a time during which all sipped at their drinks except Stout and Reno, who tossed off their liquor in a single gulp.

Will Grissom broke the quiet. "Can leave this Rye up to me and Jack, same as always. I ain't swallowing all this talk about him being such a curly wolf. Gets wet in the rain same as I do."

"Don't figure him short," Potter warned. "He ain't just

another badge-toting lawman. He stands plenty big all over the country. If something happens to him it'll draw a lot of attention."

The men considered that thoughtfully. Finally Wolcott, his small, dark eyes on Delano, spoke: "You said something about maybe this Rye had a price. If he does, can count me in for my share."

"You really figure he can be bought?" Potter asked, a doubtful strain in his voice. "From what I've heard there ain't nothing that'll touch him like that—nothing. He's as straight as he is tough."

Delano shrugged, refilled Stout and Reno's glasses. "No law says we can't find out, gentle like. A man never knows the answer to something till he asks."

"How you going to do that? Just come out plain and ask him if he's willing to back off for cash money," Reno wondered.

"A damn good way to get your head blowed off," Potter said dryly. "You sure best not try that!"

"Wasn't figuring to," Delano said. "Aim to work on what I'm hoping's his soft spot."

"A woman," Reno finished, grinning.

Delano nodded. Lefore said: "You talking about Mada Fremont?"

Again the Palo Duro's owner nodded. Nate Stout downed his whiskey, smiled broadly. "Good idea, for sure!"

Delano shrugged, finished off the liquor remaining in his glass and glanced around the saloon. One of the gamblers he'd brought in from St. Louis had a game going with three patrons in the casino area while two of the girls looked on. A small group had gathered at the chucka-luck cage nearby, while at the bar several men were engaged in an earnest discussion of some sort with Glenn. The rest of his employees—the extra barman, two girls and a trio of idle gamblers—were collected near the piano, taking their ease while they awaited the crush of business that would come with night.

"I don't see her," Delano murmured, replying to Stout's question. Raising a hand, he caught the eye of one of the girls and beckoned her to the table.

"Expect Mada's in her room. Tell her I want to see her."

The woman hurried off, disappearing through a doorway in the back that led to living quarters furnished by Delano and shared by all. Almost at once Mada Fremont appeared. Moving gracefully, she approached Delano and the others, who watched with unconcealed appreciation.

A bit more than of average height, Mada was a striking brown-eyed blonde with a well-rounded figure. She added to her natural beauty by rouging her lips and cheeks, and at the moment was wearing a bright yellow low-cut dress.

The men at the table stirred, rose politely as she halted before them. That she was no ordinary saloon girl was evident in the deference accorded her, just as it was understood that she was Ben Delano's woman.

"We've got a problem," he said in his quiet way as she sat down.

"The new sheriff," she furnished, smiling. "Why? The others have never worried you for long."

"This one—John Rye's—different," Delano explained. "He's not the ordinary kind—"

"Reckon you could say he's the top hand when it comes

to being a badge-toter," Nate Stout said. "Gets sent all over the country when some special kind of a job turns up."

"Some folks say he works direct for the President," Potter added, "but I got my doubts about that. I expect old Ruthy Hayes has got more to do than bother with lawmen."

"Probably so," Wolcott agreed, "but this Rye is a tough one, hard as all hell on outlaws and anybody else he figures is breaking the law."

"Got folks to calling him the Doomsday Marshal," Reno said, "so you can see what kind of a reputation he's built up for himself."

Mada took up the bottle of Bourbon, filled Delano's empty glass half full and drank it. Glancing about the table, she shrugged, said, "What's this got to do with me?"

"It's who and what he is that makes him a big problem," Delano began, slowly. "We've got to get rid of him, but doing it the usual way—letting Grissom and Turner take care of it—is too risky. Could mean real trouble for all of us."

"We figure to try and buy him off," Wolcott said, getting straight to the point. "We want you to get cozy with him—make him an offer."

Mada nodded thoughtfully, flicked Delano with a glance. "Won't be much of a job if—"

"We could use Renee," Vic Lefore said, referring to one of the girls at the Parisian. "She's real good at handling men special-like."

"No need for her," Mada cut in stiffly. "I can take care of this John Rye—or any other man I've ever seen. When and where do I see him and how much cash is on the line?"

"Still have to figure that out," Delano replied, "but we'll have it all set up by dark."

Jeremiah Potter wagged his head worriedly. "You best know what you're getting yourself into. This fellow Rye, he'd as soon put a bullet in you as not, and claim it was all in the line of duty."

Mada smiled, arched her full, dark brows. "I have a way with men," she said confidently.

"I think we can depend on the lady," Delano said, pushing back his chair to signify the end of the meeting. As the others, with the exception of the woman, got to their feet, he added: "I'll decide on a figure, and work out how much cash we'll each have to kick in. That agreeable?"

All members of the council but Herman Mueller responded immediately in the affirmative. Delano studied the restaurant owner briefly.

"Something about this you don't like, Dutch?"

"It is the money. I am not sure I can raise much. There has not been many customers."

"You'll only have to pay a fair share," Delano said, "and that'll be less than most of us. It'll be figured on how much business you do. Don't worry about it."

Mueller bobbed. Turning away, he hurriedly rejoined the rest of the council moving toward the door. Grissom and his shadow, Jack Turner, standing to one side, waited until the restaurant man was gone, and then the former spoke.

"You sure you want to go to all that trouble with this tin star?" he asked. "Me'n Jack can damn quick—"

"If this doesn't work, then it'll be up to you," Delano replied, and dismissed the pair by drawing his chair back into the table and putting his attention on Mada Fremont.

Before he could speak, the woman said, "You expecting me to get real close to this lawman?"

"If it's necessary—I don't think it will be."

Mada helped herself to another drink. "I thought I was all through with that."

"You are, except maybe for this one time. This Rye has put us in a bad way. We could lose everything."

The woman set her empty glass on the table, favored the saloon keeper with a half smile. "We sure don't want to do that now, do we? But don't worry, I'll make this Doomsday lawman see things my way."

CHAPTER 9

The shooting had occurred in the Kansas City, Rye saw as he turned into the street. A half a dozen men were standing in front of the building, some peering into the open doorway while others idly watched Jeremiah Potter, stretcher on his shoulder, approaching from the direction of his livery stable.

Reaching the saloon, the lawman crowded past the curious onlookers. Moving up to its entrance, he stepped inside. He halted immediately, the sudden change from the bright sunlight of the street to the dim interior of the saloon momentarily blinding him.

Reno's place was not large, Rye saw when his vision had cleared. There were a number of scarred tables with chairs, above which a chandelier made from a wagon wheel and several oil lamps hung. A half a dozen patrons were to be seen, along with Phil Reno and a number of scantily clad, worn-looking women.

Reno was sitting at one of the tables with two other men. Nearby on the floor lay a fairly well-dressed individual—obviously a gambler. As Rye entered and walked toward the group, Phil Reno got to his feet and arrogantly waved the lawman back.

"Ain't no need for you coming here, Marshal," he said.

"Tinhorn there tried cheating Rufe—so Rufe up and shot him."

Rye coldly ignored the saloon keeper. Hunching beside the gambler, he felt first for a pulse; finding none, he searched the man for a weapon, failing there also. Coming back upright, the marshal put his attention on the men at the table with Reno.

"Which one of you is Rufe?"

A small, wiry-looking man with a pock-marked face stirred lazily. "That's me—Rufe."

"Gambler wasn't armed. Why'd you have to shoot him?"

"Hell, he was cold-decking me!" Rufe replied, frowning.

"What difference it make, anyway?" Reno demanded. "That Kennedy weren't nothing but a stinking card sharp, and had it coming. Why don't you just be on your way, let us take care—"

"Stay out of this, Reno!" Rye snapped coldly. "Man's broke the law—he's going to answer for it."

"That's something I ain't about to do," the saloon owner shot back. "This here's my place, and it ain't none of your damned business what—"

"Murder is the law's business—and I'm the law," the marshal said, and glanced about at the men staring at him sullenly. "Something you had all better understand."

The incident was made to order for John Rye; he needed to demonstrate not only the presence but the strength of the law as well, and he could not have arranged a better situation had he done it personally.

"Want you to all remember this," he continued. "Man that was shot didn't have a weapon on him. That makes it murder, and could be some of you will be called to testify before a judge to that."

Testify—judge . . . The words rippled through the crowd in the saloon.

"That's right. I'm locking the killer up, and holding him for trial—"

"The hell you are!" Rufe shouted suddenly, and lunging to his feet, made a stab for the pistol on his hip.

Rye drew fast. His arm lashed out with the speed of a striking rattlesnake. The heavy six gun in his hand caught Rufe on the side of the head, dropped him back into the chair in which he had been. The pistol he'd managed to drag from its holster thudded to the floor as consciousness deserted him.

The lawman, weapon still in his hand, again glanced about. There was a stillness to him, and his narrowed eyes were colorless in the weak light.

"Anybody else want to argue the point?" he asked in a velvet-soft voice.

There was no audible response, only shuttered, hating looks. Bending down, Rye picked up the outlaw's gun and thrust it under his belt. Beckoning then to Potter standing beyond the tables, he said, "All right, get at it."

The stableman did not hesitate. Drafting a man in the crowd, he hurried to where the gambler, Kennedy, lay. Opening the stretcher, he and his assistant laid the body upon it. Then, grasping the handles and rising, they started for the doorway.

Rye waited until they had disappeared into the street. At that point he reached out, seized Rufe by his shirt front and jerked the senseless man to his feet. The outlaw's head wobbled loosely and a groan escaped his throat.

"Move back!" the lawman warned the men gathered around. Pistol ready in one hand, the other firmly gripping Rufe's shirt, he began to make his way to the saloon's entrance.

"Hold off here, damn it!" Phil Reno shouted, features working angrily. "You can't go taking—"

"You want some of what Rufe got?" the marshal asked in a hard voice as he half walked, half dragged his prisoner toward the doorway.

Reno hesitated, made no reply, simply stared. Rye, again sweeping the saloon's patrons with a warning look, stepped out into the open when he gained the entrance. The men clustered about the landing watched him stolidly.

Continuing to the center of the street, Rye paused for a firmer grip on Rufe. The outlaw's senses were still befuddled from the blow he had taken, but a degree of consciousness had returned.

"I'm warning everybody—stay out of this!" Rye called in a voice pitched to be heard the length of the street.

He was no hand at theatrics, but he felt it was necessary to show one and all that law had returned to Crisscross, and meant business.

Immediately he started down the center of the street for the jail. The distance between the Kansas City, standing as it did at the extreme north end of the town, and the jail, a good three quarters of the settlement's length in the opposite direction, made for an ideal—if unplanned—demonstration.

Persons in the Palo Duro, the Parisian, Stout's, Wolcott's, Mueller's Bluebird Restaurant, as well as any taking refuge from the sun in the several intervening vacant buildings, would witness Rufe being ignominiously dragged and alternately propelled to the lockup. Only people in Potter's Livery Stable at the south end of the street, and someone unaware of what was taking place, would miss the show.

But through it all John Rye was taking no unnecessary chances. As he strode purposefully along with his dazed prisoner, he kept the man between his body and the west side of the street where there was the most likelihood of danger. Pistol ready and clearly visible in his left hand, he maintained a sharp watch on the buildings standing on both sides of the street.

Right now he could use a bit of Aaron Burke's promised help, but the deputy was nowhere to be seen, and Rye pressed on, with Rufe beginning to struggle and resist more with each step. But the lawman's strength was irresistible, and he had little difficulty forcing the smaller outlaw toward the jail.

Glancing coolly from side to side, the marshal took satisfaction from the number of faces he saw, and smiled back grimly at the hatred that was evident on all. It was strange to receive no friendly and encouraging looks as he performed his duty, but such was to be expected, he realized. In a town populated by outlaws and their sympathizers, anything a lawman did was certain to be unpopular.

Coming abreast of the Bluebird, Rye began to angle for his office with its accompanying jail. Reaching the entrance, he gave Rufe a hard shove that sent him stumbling inside while he paused to glance back up the street.

A taut smile split his mouth. Wolcott, Nate Stout and Lefore were all hurrying toward the Palo Duro. Phil Reno was already there, and was at that moment pushing through the saloon's ornate batwings.

Another meeting was about to get underway, that was certain—one that would have to do with him, and the law that was making itself felt.

"This here's a stinking hogpen," Rufe declared as Rye relieved him of his gun belt, pushed him into one of the cells and locked the iron-bar door.

"It sure is," the lawman agreed laconically. "What's the rest of your name?"

"Custer."

"All right, Rufe Custer, you're in there for murder. I don't know when a judge'll come by here—maybe never the way this town's going—but you'll get a trial someday."

"Damned tinhorn was cheating me."

"Could be—but that didn't give you the right to gun him down. Only the law can take a man's life, and that's after he's been found guilty of a serious crime. Time you, and other owl-hoots like you, remembered that."

Custer moved away from the front of the cell and sat down on the dust-covered cot. Ruefully touching the side of his head, he produced a sly smile.

"I got plenty of friends around here. Just could be I won't be waiting for no judge," he said.

The lawman's shoulders stirred. "Best you pass the word to those friends to stay out of it, else they'll find themselves locked up in there with you—or maybe getting buried. Jailbreaking can get mighty dangerous."

Custer grinned smugly and shook his head. Rye, hearing noises behind the jail, walked the length of the hall to determine the source. Aaron Burke had been as good as his word; a woman was inside the small house giving it a badly needed cleaning.

"How about some water? It's hot in here!" Rufe called as the lawman moved past his cell. "And when am I going to get something to eat?"

"Later," Rye answered, and continued on into the office area.

Slipping Custer's pistol into its belted holster, and hanging the bit of heavy gear on a peg alongside the weapon he'd recovered from Virg Cahoon, Rye turned for a look at the room. Burke had hung his saddlebags across the back of the chair—both it and the desk had been wiped clean of dust—and stood the shotgun in the rack built onto the wall.

The marshal, deciding he'd best get the report ready he intended sending the commander at Fort Union on the ambush, dug into one of the leather pouches and produced the packets of items he'd taken off the bodies of the soldiers.

Pulling open the top drawer of the desk, Rye rustled about in its contents until he found a clean sheet of paper. With the pencil he carried in his shirt pocket he wrote an account of the killings and gold robbery as related to him by the dying Henry Exter. That completed, he advised that he had in his spare moments located the stolen army wagon and mules, but so far had no idea who the bushwhackers could be, or where they might have gone. He finished the report with the suggestion that a detail be dispatched to Crisscross immediately, where it could take up the trail before it got any colder.

Signing the letter *John Rye, Spec. U. S. Marshal,* he

rummaged through the desk drawer again until he found an unused envelope. Placing inside it the folded sheet of paper, he sealed and addressed it to the fort's commander. That finished, the lawman sighed, always relieved to get the chore of making a written report of any kind off his mind. Going into his saddlebags once more, he came up with the flour sack he sometimes used to carry grub when not trailing his pack horse. Putting the soldiers' effects inside it along with the letter, Rye tied its open end securely and laid it on one of the benches.

He would meet the stagecoach when it arrived that next morning, instruct the driver to deliver the sack to the Fort Union commander personally. At that point he would have done all he could, and all that he had promised Sergeant Exter—but that didn't mean he would not continue his own investigation as time and duty permitted.

Leaning back in the chair, Rye let his thoughts return to the wagon and the missing gold. He hadn't had time to really look things over, to see if there was anything that would help him determine who the outlaws that had ambushed the army detail might be. He'd like the chance to go back, have a thorough look around.

The mules would be no problem. He'd put that matter in the hands of Potter at the livery stable, instruct him to care for the animals until the Army arrived and took over.

Just how much time he could spend on tracking down the outlaws, however, was questionable. He had fired the opening gun, so to speak, in the war against the outlaws making Crisscross their hangout when he shot Virg Cahoon and jailed Rufe Custer—and he could expect repercussions. Such would not come from the two outlaws' friends alone, but from the men running the town as well.

They had made it clear they wanted things left as they were, and that law was unwelcome. Rye knew they'd not let this latest incident pass without a strong protest—and possibly some sort of active show of strength. Their chief attraction to the outside world was that no law existed in Crisscross, that it was free, wide open, and a town where any man could do what he wished without interference. The council had done much to publicize that fact.

Why couldn't he combine the two problems that occupied his mind? While he was keeping an eye out for wanted criminals frequenting the settlement with the intention of jailing them, and putting a stop to the hell-raising that had apparently been going on in the street, why not also be asking questions that might give him a clue as to the identities of the bushwhackers.

Rye could find no good reason to the contrary, and concluding there was no time like the present to begin operations, the lawman got to his feet and reached for the shotgun in the rack. He paused, hearing the rap of boot heels in the hall.

The thought came swiftly to him that it could be an attempt to free Rufe Custer; pivoting, he crossed to where he could see the corridor. It was Aaron Burke. Shrugging, somewhat surprised at the quick rise of tension he had experienced, Rye turned back to his desk. The deputy, wearing a holstered gun now as well as his star, slowed briefly to have his look at the prisoner, then came on into the office, his brows pulled together in a frown.

"Heard about Rufe killing that gambler, and you a'dragging him down the middle of the street to the jail.

Sure wish't I could've seen that! What do you aim to do with him?"

"Hold him for trial—the charge is murder," Rye replied, puzzled by the question. What else would he do?

"Then I reckon you'll have to trot him off to some other town. There ain't no judge going to come by here."

"Why not?"

"Gaskol told me the fellow that's supposed to come by every month or so to hold court was bought off by Delano and them—paid to just forget about this town."

Rye swore deeply. The power of money was far-reaching when it could turn a circuit judge aside and per-suade him from doing his prescribed duties.

"Means I'll take Custer to the nearest county seat, then. I'm not about to let this bunch think they can get the best of the law," Rye said. "The way it stacks up there's no elected government at all in this county."

"Nope, not any more," Burke said. "The council's the government—the whole cheese."

"What about the rest of the towns?"

"Ain't none, 'cepting a village or two. Crisscross is the only town in the whole county."

"Been that way long?"

"For quite a spell—"

"Means then you haven't drawn any pay for being a deputy."

Burke brushed at the sweat on his cheeks, shook his head. "No, but I ain't worrying none. Raise most of what I eat out at my place, and when I'm needing cash—which ain't often—I sell a little to the Dutchman."

"Could draw some pay if you'd lined up with the coun-cil as their deputy, I suppose—"

"Yeh, sure could. Same with Gaskol. But me, well, I felt the same about it as him."

Rye said, "Not right. Man deserves pay for what he does. I'll see about getting that squared away, same as I'll get a judge coming back by here. Was about to take a walk up the street—"

Burke glanced through the broken glass of the window. "It ain't long till supper. Thought maybe you'd come eat with me tonight."

Rye smiled. "Be a pleasure—if it's no trouble."

"It sure ain't no trouble," the deputy declared. "Woman friend of mine's always bringing over some victuals so's I won't have to do no cooking."

"She the same one that's cleaning up my house?"

"Nope, her sister. Stopped in there a bit ago when I come by. She's almost done. Be here in the morning to give this place a going over. That the stuff you want put on the stage for Fort Union?" Burke added, pointing to the sack lying on the bench.

"That's it, all ready to go. Had a bit of good luck—run into the wagon and mules."

The deputy's brows lifted in surprise. "That so? Where?"

"Old deserted homestead north and west of town a ways."

"That'll be the Montgomery place. Only one up there. Anybody around?"

"No, but I'll tell you all about it on the way to your house. I'm getting hungry thinking about a good, woman-cooked meal."

"Might as well start walking, then. How about the prisoner? Ain't we going to feed him?"

Rye picked up his saddlebags, intending to leave them in his living quarters as they passed by.

"Sure," he said, replying to the deputy's question. "I'll get something from the Bluebird when we get back. He'll last till then."

Burke grinned. "Yeh, reckon he will," he said, starting down the hallway. "Can maybe save you a mite of trouble, though. Mamie fixed up a lot more grub than I can use, even with company. You can bring back enough of our leavings for him when we're done."

Rye agreed. Ignoring the prisoner's protests, the two lawmen left the jail, pausing long enough for the marshal to set his saddlebags inside the house provided for his use. Crossing the stream—Dead Man's Creek, so Burke advised Rye—they traveled the half mile or so on beyond to Aaron Burke's small, farm-like home.

The meal, as the deputy had promised, was a delicious one. John Rye, a footloose man because of his profession, and therefore forever on the move, was forced to make the best of his own cooking talents while on the trail. Consequently, he truly appreciated the treat.

"Was a supper I won't soon forget," the marshal said as he and Burke, near dark, headed back for the jail.

"Sure glad you come," the deputy, carrying a plate of food for Rufe Custer, replied. "Man can sure get mighty tired of eating alone."

"I'll be pleased to come anytime I'm asked," Rye said, and slowed his step.

Burke frowned. "What's the matter? You see something?"

"The jail—the back door's open," the lawman said in a

terse voice, shifting the shotgun from the crook of his left arm to his right hand. "We left it closed."

Quickening his pace, Rye entered the building. He halted abruptly. The door to Custer's cell was standing open.

"Rufe's gone," the lawman said, facing Burke. His voice was taut, bristling with anger. "Somebody has busted him out!"

CHAPTER 10

Burke stepped in beside Rye, making an examination of the cell door. "Looks to me like whoever it was used a crowbar, just pried the lock apart."

"Broke—ruined it," the marshal agreed, and put his attention on the floor. There were a number of prints in the thick dust; crouching, he studied them closely.

"Were two men," he said after a bit. "Easy to spot my tracks—and Rufe's, tell them from the others."

Features grim set, Rye drew himself upright and walked into the office, glancing out into the street as he did. There was still some light in the sky, which would indicate the jail break, occurring earlier, had taken place at a time when anyone along the street could have seen what was happening. But there would be no one in Crisscross who would admit to being a witness, the lawman knew. Rufe Custer's friends, as well as those who did not know him but were of the same calling, would know nothing of the incident if questioned—but that was to be expected.

Rye, the lines of his face still hard set, turned to the deputy.

"Want to start looking for Rufe. Probably still in town hiding out, or getting ready to leave."

Burke had set the plate of food on one of the benches, and was thoughtfully rubbing his jaw. "Can't be no more'n an hour or so since he got busted out. He'll still be around, all right."

"Time like this it's smart to do a little bluffing," the marshal said. "Put the word out that we know what the pair that helped him looked like—just don't know their names." Shotgun back in the crook of his left arm, Rye gave the deputy a critical glance. "That gun you're wearing shoot?"

Burke said, "Sure," and grasping the butt of the pistol on his hip, raised the weapon slightly, then let it slip back into the holster. "Had to kill me a snake last week with it. How you want to do this?"

"Whoever it was that helped Rufe will want him to lay low, or get out of town fast—which is what they'll prefer. Easier to keep their noses clean if he's not around. Where do you figure he's been doing his sleeping?"

Burke frowned, again scratched at his jaw. "Hard to tell, but most of his kind've been laying out in one of the empty buildings along the street, and keeping their horses in some shed close by."

"Makes sense, so that's the place to start—the empty buildings. You take the street, I'll work the alley, east side, till we get to the Parisian. If we don't flush him out by then, we'll cross over and double back on the west side. If we still haven't jumped him, we'll make the saloons together."

"Got a hunch we'll find Rufe before it comes to that," Burke said as they stepped out into the darkening street. "Was thinking—might be best was I to do my looking behind the buildings. I sort of know the places where Rufe's most liable to be."

"Suit yourself," Rye said, after giving the idea brief

thought. And then added as they separated, the deputy swinging off to the right on his way to the alley, "Yell out if you jump him. Don't try taking him yourself."

Burke nodded, and continued on his way. Rye, moving on, gained the first of the vacant store buildings and moved quietly up to the open doorway. Glancing inside, he saw quickly that the small structure was empty. Waiting there until he saw Aaron Burke had come abreast in the alley at the opposite end of the building, the marshal resumed his search.

The fact that he had never lost a prisoner was a matter of personal pride with John Rye, and to have it happen for the first time in a town where he was endeavoring to establish law and make it meaningful increased by double or more the necessity for recapturing the outlaw and locking him in a cell again.

The marshal found no one in any of the succeeding vacant buildings, nor did Burke, and together they reached Mueller's Bluebird Restaurant. Passing on by it, they came to the structure that had housed the Bonanza. Two drifters were asleep inside the doorless, large and apparently once prominent saloon, and Rye, without awakening them, stood quietly by until he had received a signal from Burke that all was clear at his end of the premises.

It was steadily growing darker, and Rye was anxious to get the east side of the street canvassed before night settled in fully. They drew a blank at the empty building standing between the old Bonanza and Nate's Gun & Saddle Shop. This left but one more deserted structure remaining before reaching Vic Lefore's Parisian.

There was lamplight showing in Stout's place as Rye

passed, pausing only momentarily to glance through the small window that faced the street. Stout evidently had living quarters in the rear, and likely was having his evening meal at the time.

"Here!"

Burke's sudden and frantic shout brought the lawman up short. It had come from the rear of the empty building beyond Stout's. Moving fast, Rye rounded the corner of the gun and saddle shop. Midway, the blast of a pistol shattered the hush. The marshal swore, rushed on. He shouldn't have permitted Aaron Burke to take on the responsibility, as inexperienced as he apparently was, of going after a killer like Rufe alone; he should have kept the man at his side.

Gaining the alley-like area, Rye slowed. Burke was standing near a shed at the rear of the vacant building. A partly saddled horse was tethered to a post at its corner. Close by, stretched out on the dusty ground and apparently dead, was Rufe Custer.

Lights were beginning to show in the windows of the Parisian, and voices in the street could be heard as Rye hurriedly joined the deputy.

"Told him—Rufe—to hold it," Burke said in a strained, agitated voice. "Grabbed for his gun—already had mine out so I—I shot him."

Rufe Custer undoubtedly was the first man the deputy had ever shot, and it was affecting him deeply. These were the moments, Rye knew, when a good lawman was made or lost. The times and the nature of the outlaws with whom they were forced to contend ruled out all consideration for the faint of heart or those who harbored any degree of fear for their future.

And fear was what John Rye saw in the eyes of Aaron Burke. The deputy was realizing what he had done and the consequences thereof; Rufe's friends, probably all shootists of long standing, would certainly be out to avenge his death as befit the code, and Aaron knew he would not stand a chance against them.

"Holster that pistol," Rye ordered.

The thud of running boots could be heard as men from the nearby saloons came to see what the shooting was about. There were sounds at Stout's place, too, as if Nate was intending to investigate the disturbance.

"Listen to me," the marshal said sternly. "It was me that shot Rufe, understand? Nobody saw what happened, so nobody'll know any better."

Relief was evident in the deputy's manner and voice. He nodded. "Sure, but it ain't right—you taking the blame for—"

Rye, handing the shotgun to Burke, drew his own pistol. "Better my way," he said, coming up with a quick and sensible reason for assuming the responsibility that offered a way out for the deputy. "I'll be riding on soon, but you live here."

"Who was it?" a man rounding the corner of the Parisian called, and then seeing Rye and Burke, slowed his step. He was joined by two others coming also from the street beyond the Parisian.

"It's that marshal. He's killed hisself another'n!"

Nate Stout emerged from the back door of his establishment. Rye considered the merchant coldly as he came in close.

"That's Rufe Custer," the lawman said clearly, letting it

be known who the dead man was without further delay. "Broke jail while I was having supper with Burke. We went hunting for him, found him saddling up to leave."

"It's Rufe sure enough," one of the growing crowd announced.

"I reckon he didn't have no chance against that marshal," another onlooker lamented.

"He got what he asked for," Rye said coldly. "Rufe was in jail for murder, and escaped. When he did that he knew he was in for trouble—the kind you can only get out of by using a gun. Same goes for the two men who helped him."

"Hell, did you have to kill him?" a cowhand, apparently just in off the range—judging from his sweaty, dusty look—asked in a falling voice.

"It was him that made the decision to shoot it out," Rye replied, and pointed to the pistol still in the dead man's grasp. "One of you go get Potter, tell him to come take care of the body."

"Your job—it ain't up to me," someone said.

The sullen comment was echoed by a murmur of agreement. A hard grin parted the lawman's lips, and he stepped forward quickly, prepared to commandeer by force if necessary the services of one of the bystanders. Words from Jeremiah Potter checked him.

"Reckon I'm already here, Mr. Marshal," the stable owner said in a dry, flat and friendless way.

Rye shrugged, turned his back on the man and faced Burke.

"Can mark off the escaped prisoner," he said callously. "Next job's to find the pair who helped him break out.

Expect the Kansas City'll be a good place to start asking questions."

Aaron Burke made no reply, but numbly fell in beside the marshal as he moved into the passageway lying between the Parisian and the empty building.

CHAPTER 11

Reaching the street, Rye halted. It was evident the word of Rufe's killing, carried by one of the bystanders, had preceded him and the deputy, for in the pools of light cast by lamps on the fronts of the saloons, groups of men had gathered. Other buildings, the vacant as well as the occupied, except for the Bluebird Restaurant, were dark.

"The shooting seems to have stirred things up more'n it ought," the lawman said. "My guess is there was a lot of talking about us and Rufe going on before it even happened."

Burke offered no reply, and this drew Rye's close attention. The strain had not disappeared from the deputy's taut features, and a nervous tension was shaking his slender frame.

"Expect it'd be smart for you to go on home, take the rest of the night off," Rye said, reaching for the shotgun Burke was holding. "You look a mite wore out."

At such times it was good to have a backup man with him, the lawman knew, but it should be one upon whom he could depend completely. Having a man in Aaron Burke's present frame of mind would be worse than none at all; such would call for not only looking out for his own skin but that of the deputy's as well.

"I'll be all right—fine," Burke said, struggling to steady

his voice. "It's only that I ain't never—well, I ain't been no deputy for long, and this here's the first time I've ever used my gun on a man—killed him."

"Always tough facing up to how you feel—"

Burke nodded, rubbed agitatedly at the back of his neck. "Hell, I ain't sure now I'm cut out for this kind of work," he said, staring at the small crowd in front of the Palo Duro, directly opposite.

"Some men aren't."

"Know damn well I'd not be able to stand up to some of them gunhands of Rufe's when they come looking to even up the killing."

"You won't have to, long as you keep your mouth shut and let things stand the way they are," Rye said. "Now, trot on home. I'll see you in the morning."

"What I aim to do . . . Marshal, can I ask you a question?"

"Sure."

"When you shoot a man—kill him, I mean—don't it sort of chaw on you?"

Rye was quiet for several moments. Then, "I've learned to live with it," he said. "Important thing, far as your conscience is concerned, is don't ever kill a man unless he forces your hand."

Burke nodded. "Helps some knowing you feel it, too. G'night—have a care," he added as he turned away.

"Figure to," the marshal replied. Cradling the shotgun, he crossed the street, ignoring the men in front of Delano's Palo Duro, and strode toward the adjacent Kansas City.

There were three loungers on the porch as Rye approached the structure. Giving them a sharp glance, he walked by through the open doorway and entered the saloon, better lit now by several bracketed wall lamps aiding the overhead chandeliers. There were a dozen or more customers present in addition to Phil Reno, the bartender and several women. Reno made no show of welcome when he saw the lawman, simply remained at the end of the bar where he was in conversation with two friends, and sullenly watched the lawman draw near.

"Rufe Custer's dead," Rye stated flatly, halting in front of the saloonkeeper. "I reckon you know that."

Reno's thick shoulders stirred indifferently. "So?"

"I'm looking for the two jaspers that busted him out of jail," the lawman said, and glanced about at the now hushed crowd. "Don't know their names, only what they look like. You can save the law a lot of time if you'll speak up, say who they are."

Phil Reno smiled, turned to the saloon's patrons. "Anybody here want to give the marshal a hand?"

Rye knew there would be no affirmative response—at least there in front of witnesses—but there just could be someone with a grudge against one or both of the men he was looking for, or that deep down had a spark of respect for law and order, who might get word to him on the sly later.

Where John Rye was concerned, the upholding of the law was what counted, and he believed in pursuing such by any means and manner available to him. The important factor here, he felt, was to let it be known that the law was not allowing the jail break to pass without drastic action being taken, that every effort would be made to find, arrest, jail and hold for trial the men who helped Rufe Custer.

"You're wasting your time, Marshal," Reno drawled after a time when only silence was the answer to the question he had asked. "And, I'd as soon you'd get the hell out of here. You sort of make my customers fidgety."

Rye smiled bleakly and again glanced about, the muzzle of the shotgun he held drifting aimlessly over the crowd.

"When I'm finished," he said. "Rufe hung around here. Makes me think his friends are here, too."

"Maybe so—I sure wouldn't know," Reno said. Then, shifting his attention to his customers again, he asked in a mocking tone, "Any of you folks real friendly with Rufe?"

A ripple of laughter followed the question. A man in a rumpled, sweat-stained suit and derby hat, sitting at one of the tables, rocked forward unsteadily.

"Is he that there little fat fellow they call Sandy Claus?"

There were more laughs, and another customer then said, "If that's him, he sure ain't no friend of mine. The sonofabitch brung me a sock full a hay one Christmas, and I been hating his guts ever since!"

Rye, silent throughout the snide commenting, waited until it was quiet once more. "Something else I'm looking for—somebody who saw an army wagon pulled by four mules come by here yesterday, or maybe the day before that. Could have been a half a dozen riders with it."

"What's the matter, Marshal? You tired of lawing and figuring to join the Army?"

Rye shrugged off the disparaging question. "Important I talk to anybody who did—"

"Hell, Marshal, there ain't nobody going to give you

any help around here," Reno cut in. "If you had any sense you'd seen that by now."

"Maybe I have," Rye said coolly, "but every man under this roof had better get this straight—the law has come back to this two-bit town, and the sooner they realize that and start working with it, the less chance they'll have of winding up dead and in the boneyard like Rufe Custer!"

Wheeling slowly, Rye retraced his steps to the doorway, fully aware of the heavy silence he left behind. He knew there was more than one man present in the saloon who was yearning to put a bullet in his back, but he was relying on sheer bravado, and the intimidating muzzle of the double-barreled shotgun he carried, to forestall any such effort.

Reaching the porch, really little more than a landing, the marshal halted. There were only two loafers there now; touching them a second time with a hard, narrow look, he stepped down into the loose dust and struck off through the gloom for the Palo Duro, the Kansas City's neighbor to the south.

Ben Delano kept his place of business well lighted. There were three large chandeliers and at least a dozen wall lamps to dispel the darkness and lend an air of gaiety to the saloon. There were at least triple the number of patrons the lawman had noted in the Kansas City—one of whom was Nate Stout—and all were amusing themselves at the card tables and gambling devices, or were bellied up to the bar enjoying their liquor.

Several brightly clad women were moving among the customers seeing to their wants. Over near the piano, which was adding its music to the low, steady din filling the saloon, a freshly scrubbed and shaved cowhand in clean shirt, pants and boots with badly run-over heels, still wearing his stained hat, was stomping out a clog in the smoky atmosphere with a girl in a red dress.

Rye, having stopped and stepped aside within the batwings, gave the large room a slow survey, finally locating Delano at a table in a back corner not far from the bar. Making his way through the crowd, he wondered as he did how the most recent meeting he had seen shaping up had gone. The saloon man was alone, and at that moment was writing something in a small pocket-ledger. He glanced up as Rye halted before him.

"Evening, Marshal," he greeted genially.

Rye nodded slightly. Delano was a cool, quiet sort of man, strictly self-controlled, and difficult to figure out exactly. He could be, the lawman thought, the most dangerous man in Crisscross.

"Something I can do for you?"

"Rufe Custer's dead," Rye answered. "Probably not news to you."

"No, I heard about it. Was trying to escape, leave town, I understand."

"Right. What I want now is the two men who pried open one of my cells and let him loose," Rye said. Turning, he moved to the end of the bar. Gaining the attention of the crowd by thumping on the counter with the butt of his shotgun, the lawman repeated the statements and declarations he'd made earlier in the Kansas City. As in the smaller saloon, there was no response, only a sullen hush.

Rye rode out the silence for a good two minutes and then, in a contemptuous tone, said, "Figured as much

from you, but you best get used to me being around looking after the law, because we're both here to stay."

Pivoting, the marshal moved back to where Ben Delano
was sitting. There was an attractive blond woman with
him now, one dressed in a low-cut, yellow dress. She favored Rye with a wide, friendly smile. Acknowledging
the greeting, the lawman centered on Delano again.

"I expect you to speak up if you know who that pair
was. Jailbreaking's a mighty serious offense, and this time
it got the man they busted loose killed."

Delano shrugged, brushed at the moisture collected
along his mustache. There was a faint breeze stirring
through the building, thanks to several open windows
and the doors, but it did little to lessen the heat.

"Be glad to do what you're asking, Marshal," Delano
said, "if I knew who they were. Same goes for that army
wagon and team of mules you're asking about. I certainly
didn't see them, and I haven't listened to anybody talking
about it." He paused, seeing a frown on the marshal's
face.

"Are you surprised at me for knowing you were going
to ask about that wagon?" the saloon keeper continued
with a smile. "Don't be, Marshal. There's very little that
takes place around here that I don't know of fast—almost
as soon as it happens, in fact."

Delano's talebearers did move fast, Rye had to admit.
His query concerning the stolen wagon had been voiced
in the Kansas City less than a half hour previous!

"But back to that wagon you're hunting for—chances
are it passed by here during the night, and in this town at
night everybody's either in bed or inside one of the saloons enjoying themselves. But I'm forgetting my man-

ners. Marshal Rye, I'd like for you to meet a lovely lady, Miss Mada Fremont."

The lawman, shotgun now in the crook of his left arm, removed his flat-crowned hat with his right hand and bowed slightly.

"My pleasure, ma'am."

"Mada is sort of a partner of mine," Delano went on. "She's not one of the girls who work here."

The marshal smiled briefly, indicating that he understood the arrangement.

"The Town Council met today," Delano continued. "We—"

"Twice, I think it was," Rye observed dryly.

"Yes, I guess it was, but I'm talking about late today. We don't think you had any call to arrest Rufe Custer for shooting that tinhorn."

"He broke the law, and seeing to it that he went to jail for it is my job," Rye said coldly. "It'll be a right good idea if you and the rest of the council will tend to your business, and let me take care of mine."

"Sure, sure," the saloon keeper said hurriedly. "To look after law and order—that's why you were sent here. Whether that was necessary or not is a matter of opinion, but the point is we're afraid that your jailing Rufe will cause us all a lot of trouble."

"He's dead," Rye stated flatly, "why fret over him? The man broke the law and paid for doing it."

Delano looked at Mada Fremont, smiled and came back to the lawman. Elsewhere amid the thickening smoke and blending odors filling the saloon, activities had quickly resumed.

"Agreed. Rufe is out of it, but jailing him riled some of

the men—customers—plenty. I'm afraid the council can't be responsible for anything they may do. You've got to understand that they come here—sometimes from a long distance—to blow off steam and have themselves a good time. They just don't want the law around cramping their fun."

John Rye smiled crookedly. "Well, they've got it, and as far as you and the council are concerned, I'm not expecting you to be responsible. The law is my job, and I can handle it. Evening, ma'am, was nice meeting you," he added to the woman. Touching the brim of his hat with a forefinger, he returned to the street.

CHAPTER 12

More riders were coming in, arriving in singles, pairs and small groups, and the number of horses lined up at the various hitchracks was steadily increasing. That Crisscross was a popular watering hole for a wide area was evident.

Rye was conscious of the sharp scrutiny of many as he crossed over to the Parisian, and caught the disapproving mutterings of some who took immediate offense when they noted the star he was wearing. The lawman coolly ignored all. Stepping up onto the porch fronting the Parisian, he paused. The plinking of a piano, a quavering voice rendering a plaintive ballad, and the sounds of laughter and talking were coming from beyond the barrier that stood a step or two inside the open doorway and blocked the view of anyone in the street.

Rye passed through the entrance, circled the barrier and stepped into the noisy, fairly well-lit room. The Parisian had far more patrons than the Palo Duro or the Kansas City, the lawman saw, probably because it was less a saloon and more a bawdy house. There was a small bar, a few tables where cards could be played, and an area set aside near the piano for dancing. Mostly, however, the room appeared to be a large parlor with chairs and couches scattered about where customers could sit and drink and talk with one of the several scantily dressed women.

Rye, barely noticed in the smoky confusion, made his way to the bar where he saw Vic Lefore assisting the bartender in serving drinks. The saloon man caught sight of the lawman working his way through the crowd, and welcomed him with a smile and an invitation.

"Have a drink on the house, Marshal!" he called.

Rye nodded. "I'll have the drink—but I'll pay for it."

The smiled faded somewhat from Lefore's lips, but he said nothing, simply filled a glass for Rye and made change for the silver dollar the lawman laid on the counter.

"This a business call or are you here for pleasure?" Lefore asked then in his rich, southern accent. "If it's pleasure, I've got a mighty cute little Frenchie. Name's Renee—says she's from Paris. I can promise you she will show you—"

"Obliged," the marshal cut in, "but I'm here on business." Then he repeated the words he'd voiced at the two other saloons.

"I know about Rufe getting wiped out by you," Lefore said. "Some of my girls heard the shot and looked out of their windows, but I sure don't know who it was that got him out of your jail."

Rye nodded. As in the other saloons, he had expected no more. Wheeling slowly, drink in his hand, the shotgun now at his side, he looked about the room. His eyes halted briefly on two men at one of the tables—Frank Wolcott and the gunman Will Grissom. Two of the Parisian's girls were with them.

Wolcott did not speak, merely returned the lawman's

glance with a cold stare while he absently twirled his glass of liquor between a thumb and forefinger. Grissom's attention was not diverted from the woman for even a moment.

"This little lady's Renee, the one I was telling you about."

At Lefore's voice, Rye swung back around and faced the saloon keeper—and a small, ivory-skinned girl with black hair and eyes. She was smiling as she fingered a gold, heart-shaped locket suspended about her neck.

"My pleasure, monsieur," she said, raising her voice a bit to be heard. "I can make you most happy—"

"Another time, maybe," Rye said, returning the smile. Switching back to Lefore, he brought up the question of the army wagon.

As had been the case with Reno and Ben Delano, the saloon man could give Rye no help, declaring that he had seen no signs of the vehicle with its team of mules, and that he'd not heard any talk of such among his patrons.

Rye accepted Vic Lefore's statement with the same cynicism as he had the other saloon men, neither believing nor disbelieving. Setting aside his empty glass, he silenced the hubbub with a pistol shot into the floor. In the startled silence that followed, he voiced again his questions relative to the identities of the two men who had aided Rufe Custer, and the arrival of the army wagon—once more purposely avoiding any mention of where the vehicle was hidden.

As before, no help was forthcoming from the people in the crowd, who almost immediately resumed whatever activity they had been engaged in when interrupted.

Lefore considered the lawman slyly, a half grin on his

dark features. "You can see these boys ain't much interested in law—or anything like that. They're the kind that works hard all day so's they can come here and enjoy themselves at night."

"I've got no quarrel with that," the marshal said, replacing the spent cartridge in the cylinder of his pistol, "but two men helped Custer bust out of my jail, and I want them. Nobody spits in the face of the law and gets away with it while I'm around."

Lefore turned his eyes to Renee. He had removed his coat in deference to the heat, released the string tie, and now the collar of his ruffled white shirt was open. The girl met his gaze, and admitting she had aroused nothing more than a polite interest in the lawman, shrugged and moved off into the crowd.

"If I hear anything, Marshal, I will get word to you," Lefore said, an invitation for the lawman to leave definite in his voice.

Rye nodded. "Sure, sure," he murmured, dismissing the promise for what he felt it was worth. With the shotgun again in the crook of his left arm, he doubled back through the crowd to the doorway.

As he stepped out onto the porch, a warning surged through him. He had realized instantly that there was a change; no one was standing on the landing, or even in the street nearby. He was alone in the circle of light thrown by the lamps on either side of the Parisian's entrance.

Immediately Rye lunged to his right, throwing himself into the darkness beyond the lamplight. In that same fraction of time, a gun flared from the shadows beneath a nearby tree, filling the night with its sharp crack. Rye triggered his shotgun at the orange flash in the blackness. A yell of pain went up, followed by the sound of a body falling and of a weapon striking the ground. Immediately there came the quick beat of heels receding into the night.

The lawman drew himself erect, shotgun still leveled and ready. He swore harshly. There had been two bush-whackers, and one had got away.

Men and women were crowding out onto the porch of the Parisian, attracted by the deafening blast of the dou-ble-barrel so close to its entrance. Across the street at the Palo Duro, and a bit farther on at the Kansas City, the shots had been heard also, and were drawing interest but to a lesser degree.

"Another'n for Jeremiah," someone said, walking to-ward the tree. "This here new marshal's sure keeping him busy."

"Who is it?" a woman's voice asked.

Rye, stepping down off the porch, started toward the figure lying under the tree, and the group gathering about it.

"It's Sam Whitman! Now why'd you reckon he'd take a pot shot at the marshal?"

"Likely he was one of the pair that broke Rufe Custer out of jail," Rye said, supplying an answer as he halted near the dead man. The charge of buckshot had struck Whitman in the chest, doing fearful damage and bringing instantaneous death.

"Sure did tear him up," a man standing across from Rye said, accusation in his voice. "That damned scatter-gun, it ain't right to shoot somebody—"

"Forget it," the lawman cut in. "What difference does it make how a man gets himself killed? Dead's dead."

Undoubtedly Whitman was one of the two men he sought—both of whom had taken it in mind to end his search for them by setting up an ambush outside the Parisian. That there were those who knew them and could furnish the identity of the other was evidenced by the fact that the porch in front of the saloon had cleared to give the killers an open field.

Bending down, Rye had a closer look at the dead man's features. Whitman's face was familiar. He had seen him earlier in the Kansas City, he thought, or maybe it had been the Palo Duro—not that it mattered at this point.

Glancing around at the crowd, now beginning to disperse, he said, "I want the name of the other man that was in on this. I know damn well some of you saw who he was."

There was no response. Rye's jaw hardened. So far he hadn't succeeded in establishing the fear of the law that he knew was necessary in the people frequenting Crisscross. Otherwise, by now he would be getting co-operation.

"Bucking me won't get any of you anything but trouble," he continued. "If you know who he is, you'd be smart to speak up now—or down at my office, later, if you're a mite bashful about doing it."

"There ain't nobody going to do that," a husky-looking man leaning against the tree said. "We ain't about to do the law no favors, so why don't you just fork your bronc and get on out of town. We for damn sure don't want you around here!"

A mutter of concurrence came from the persons

grouped around the speaker. Rye shrugged, glanced to one side as he saw someone approaching. It was Potter, a stretcher on his shoulder.

"No town can live without the law," the marshal said. "Sooner or later it will kill itself off. Keeping this one from doing just that is why I'm here—and you can bank on me staying."

"Even if you have to shoot down every man in it," the squat man said sarcastically.

A stir of anger brightened John Rye's eyes as he turned away. "If that's what it'll take," he said brusquely, and walked on.

There was no light now in Nate's Gun & Saddle Shop, and the general store was also in darkness. A lantern hung in the entrance to Potter's Livery Stable, and a glow in the window of the Bluebird Restaurant indicated that Herman Mueller was still open for business. Other than those two, and the saloons, Crisscross showed no signs of life.

Striding along the sidewalk, taking advantage of the shadows that hung close to the buildings so as not to expose himself any more than necessary to the bushwhacker still lurking about, Rye struck for the restaurant. He wasn't hungry, not after the meal he had enjoyed at Aaron Burke's table, but a cup of coffee would taste good, and he had a desire to talk to Mueller, feel the man out, see if he could determine the restaurant owner's true sentiments.

As he walked along, fully on the alert for any untoward sounds or movements, Rye wondered who the other would-be assassin might be. Whitman, he was certain, had been in one of the saloons earlier that evening. Like as not, the man who had hurried off into the night, doubtless unnerved by the shocking blast of the shotgun, had been with Whitman at the time.

The lawman scoured his mind, struggled to recall more of Whitman, but found it useless; there had been so many faces he had looked into during his tour of the town's saloons that isolating one in his memory—other than those he'd met and now knew personally—was an impossibility.

Four men swung into view beyond the livery stable. Riding abreast, they headed for the Palo Duro and the other like establishments at the opposite end of the street. Rye stopped in the shadows, watched them draw near— all laughing and talking in anticipation of what lay ahead for them—and pass on by. All were armed, as was about every man in town, the marshal noted.

Continuing, he crossed the front of the defunct Bonanza and reached the entrance to Mueller's place. A screen door protected the restaurant from flies and other bothersome insects. Pulling it open, the lawman entered.

A large, rawboned woman of probable Nordic ancestry looked up from a stack of dishes she was wiping and greeted him with no change of expression.

"Yes?" she asked as he sat down at one of the tables.

"I could use a cup of coffee," Rye replied.

The woman—Mueller's wife, the lawman assumed— took up a china container, settled it in a deep saucer. Going back into the kitchen area, separated from the front by a wooden partition, she filled it from a granite pot sitting on the stove. She had a moment's conversation with someone that he could not see since they were behind the separating panel, and then returned. Wordlessly, she placed the cup of black, steaming liquid before him, wheeled and disappeared into the kitchen.

Shortly, a girl, somewhere in her early twenties with a ruddy round face and a plump, sturdy body, came out from behind the partition. This would be the Muellers' daughter, Rye guessed. She halted behind the counter extending across one end of the room, and in complete frankness studied him gravely as if wanting to register him well on her mind.

Mueller himself put in an appearance at that moment, hurrying forward, drying his big hands on his apron as he approached.

"Good evening, Marshal," he said in his thick, Germanic accent. "You are wanting supper? We are closing, but for you—"

"Coffee'll be all," Rye said, "and a bit of help."

At the lawman's words, Mueller's wife came from behind the partition. Her features were stiff with worry, and the daughter's eyes now had become bright with resentment.

Mueller slid a look at his wife. "Help? I—I—do not know, Marshal," he said haltingly. "It is best I—"

"Two men went into the jail while I was having supper at Aaron Burke's house, pried open a cell door and let my prisoner escape. I caught him later."

"Killed him—is that not right?" the woman cut in.

Rye nodded. "It was his choice, same as it was with Whitman—one of the pair that broke jail for Custer."

"You have killed another man?" she asked in a rising voice. "That is what the shooting was about?"

"It was," Rye answered coolly.

Why was Mueller's wife so agitated? There had been

other killings in Crisscross, he was certain—two of which had been lawmen.

The woman sighed deeply. "These terrible shootings, will they not stop?"

"Someday—when folks start siding with the law, and don't back off when they're asked to help," Rye said quietly. "That's what I'm up against now. Breaking Rufe Custer out of jail was against the law, and I'm looking for the other man that was in on it."

He paused, took a swallow of coffee and glanced through the restaurant's window at the jail, almost directly opposite. Inside it a light had suddenly blossomed. It was Aaron Burke. The marshal watched as the deputy began to work at cleaning and straightening the office.

"I haven't been able to get any help from anybody in this town, other than Burke," Rye continued. "You people aren't like Delano and the others. I figured you might want to do your part in getting the law established here again."

Again Rye hesitated, allowed his words to fully register on the Muellers. The restaurant owner was a member of the council, but he appeared to be so reluctantly. If he could somehow gain the man's confidence, persuade him to co-operate, it would be a step in the right direction.

"It is best we mind our own business," the older woman said. "We do not want trouble."

Ignoring her words, the lawman said, "Whoever the other man was that helped Custer escape was with Whitman when he took a shot at me. Ran off into the dark before I could get a look at him—or shoot."

"He did not run by here," Mueller said, finally finding his voice.

"Wasn't thinking he did, but your restaurant is right across from the jail—you get a good look at it from the window. One of you must have seen Whitman and his partner when they went in to get Custer."

"No," Mrs. Mueller said quickly. "We see nothing, none of us. We see nothing."

The lawman studied the restaurant man closely. "Is that the truth—you didn't notice who it was?"

The daughter half turned as if intending to speak. Immediately the older woman said, "We have been busy. We have seen nothing at your jail, Marshal."

Rye's mouth pulled down into a hard grin. The Muellers—most likely the girl—had seen Whitman and his partner when they entered the jail, he was dead sure, but it was evident they were afraid to speak out.

"Nobody'll ever hear about it if there's anything you want to tell me," he said. "And it's wrong to hold back any information that would help me—help the law—put a criminal in jail where he belongs."

Herman Mueller's shoulders lifted and settled resignedly. "I am sorry, Marshal. I would like to help—"

"It's mighty important for this town that I find this man and hold him for trial, like I was doing Custer. We need to let everybody know that in Crisscross nobody gets away with breaking the law in any way."

Rye finished off his coffee, cold now, set his cup back in its saucer and waited. Seconds passed, ran into minutes. The Muellers remained motionless, impassive. Finally the lawman stirred, reached into a pocket for a coin, and laying it on the table beside the empty cup, got to his feet.

It was clear he'd get no help from the Mueller family. Under ordinary circumstances they no doubt would do what they could to help, particularly Herman. But as it was, fear had the upper hand over them, and they had no confidence in the ability of the law to protect them. Such was nothing new to John Rye, and he understood their position fully. All too many times the law had failed to prove itself capable of dealing with the outlaw element.

Moving toward the door, Rye slowed, came half about. "I'm obliged to you, anyway," he said in a regretful tone.

"It is not easy, this life," Mueller said.

"I know. I expect you've got a right to be scared, and I can't fault you for it. But somewhere along the line you're going to have to decide what's right and what's wrong, make a choice, and then take a stand if you're ever to have a decent and safe place to live. Good night."

The lawman's words evoked no comment from the Muellers. Continuing out into the cooling night, he halted, threw his glance into the direction of the saloons. From the welter of sounds emanating from them, he reckoned business was at its height.

Stepping down into the ankle-deep dust, Rye started across the street, noticing as he did three men standing in front of the Parisian. A light now shone inside the general store, and he heard the eerie, quavering cry of a loon somewhere in the distant backwater of Dead Man's Creek.

CHAPTER 13

Burke looked around through the haze of yellow dust. "Was setting in my kitchen thinking when I heard them gunshots. Took out of there soon as I could pull my pants on. You all right?"

Rye nodded, crossed to the rack and placed the shotgun in one of the notches. "Bullet missed me a bit. Went into the wall, I think."

Burke wiped at his mouth with the back of a hand. "Seen Whitman. That scatter-gun sure messed him up a'plenty. What about the other jasper? Somebody said he went running off into the dark. You have any luck chasing him down?"

"None," Rye said, glancing about. The office was beginning to shape up, take on the appearance of a lawman's headquarters.

"Made all three of the saloons, asked if anybody could give me any names—got no answer. Was when I left the Parisian that Whitman and his friend took a shot at me."

"You wasn't expecting anybody to talk up, was you?"

"No, but I figured maybe somebody might pass a name to us—on the sly."

"That what you were doing there in the Bluebird, asking questions?"

Rye removed his hat, stood back against the wall. "Yeh

—being right across the street, I thought they might have seen Whitman and the other fellow come in here, assuming they didn't use the back door."

"Could have. We left it open. I'm betting the Dutchman and his frau told you no."

"Just what they did. I'm pretty sure the girl saw something, but they're all too scared to speak up."

Burke, leaning on his broom, shrugged. "Hell, you can't blame them. Like I said, I don't think Herman wanted to be a partner in this deal with Delano and them in the first place—just sort of got roped into it, and they're too scared to try and get out of it."

"Just the way I see it, and it's no pat on the back for me," Rye said, a trace of bitterness in his voice as he stared off into the street, dark now except for the area of the saloons. "Haven't done much of a job far as getting law back into this town."

Burke again brushed at his mouth. The dust raised by his broom had pretty well settled, leaving a thinner film on the freshly wiped desk, chairs and benches.

"You ain't give it time enough," the deputy said. "You're just plain asking too much, and you best keep in mind there ain't hardly nobody around that wants law— just the folks living out on the flats and in the hills that used to do their trading here, and maybe the Muellers."

Rye reached into a pocket for his cigar case. Burke refused when offered one, but the lawman, drawing forth one of the slim black stogies, bit off its ends. Bending over the lamp chimney, he puffed the weed into glowing life. For several long moments he continued to stare off into the night, not in the direction of the saloons, but at the star-filled void beyond the structures on the opposite side of the street. Finally he stirred, and removing the cigar from between his teeth, faced Burke.

"Things like this have happened before, and it always gets under my hide when folks start wondering if there's any point to establishing law in a town where nobody wants it. Hell, that doesn't count! Any town is a part of civilization, and has to become a piece of the whole, no matter what."

Burke nodded. "For sure, and don't you go fretting about a lot of folks not wanting this to be a decent town again. You don't see them around now, but you get things straightened out and they'll come moving back plenty fast."

Rye gave the older man's words consideration, smiled faintly. "Usually do . . . you feeling up to snuff again?"

Burke said, "Yeh, reckon so. There much talk around about it—about Rufe getting killed, I mean?"

"The usual, and you're in the clear. Nobody doubts that it was me. I'm a prize killer, if you believe what's being said."

The deputy laughed. "I bet you'll be losing a lot of sleep over that kind of talk!"

Again the marshal smiled. "Not likely. Did get a better chance to size up Delano and the others when I made a round of the saloons tonight."

"That mean you're changing your mind about some?"

"No, just savvy them better. Can see now that Delano and Lefore are old heads at the game—real smooth talkers, tried to make me think they were ready to go along, do anything I asked. Reno's different. Hates my guts and let me know it. Same goes for Wolcott and

Stout. Not sure about Potter. I think there's a chance he—and Mueller—could be swung over to our side."

"If any of them can, it'll be them," Burke agreed.

The marshal puffed slowly on his stogie for a bit, exhaled a cloud of smoke and studied it thoughtfully. "There anybody around here you can get to paint signs?" he asked.

Aaron scratched at his jaw. "Well, yeh, a fellow living up past me used to do work around town when things was going. Ain't seen him lately, but I expect he's still there. Why?"

"Came to me earlier when I was walking down the street and saw some riders come in, all armed. Maybe that's the key to getting things squared around here—make it unlawful to carry a gun inside the town limits. It's worked in other places, no reason why it won't here."

"Just might do the job. Sure be one way of making everbody realize we've got law here again. What do you want said on them signs?"

Rye thought back, recalling one he had seen in a distant settlement. "Have him put: CARRYING FIREARMS STRICTLY FORBIDDEN. We'll need five of them, one to nail up at the door of each of the saloons, and one for each end of the street. Like to have them soon as possible, tomorrow if he can do it."

Burke shook his head. "I ain't even sure the fellow's still around, but if he is I'll get him to do his best."

"Expect if he's gone the two of us can paint them up ourselves. Maybe won't be fancy, but they'll serve the purpose. Thought you were getting that woman to clean up in here."

"Was what I aimed to do," Burke replied, continuing to

rest his weight on the broom handle, "but like I told you, I was setting around the house in my drawers, a'stewing about letting you take the blame for shooting Rufe Custer, and in no way of a'mind to go to bed when the shooting started.

"Figured maybe you was needing me, so I got there soon as I could. It was all over howsomever, so I come on here because I sure wasn't sleepy then. Just naturally grabbed myself a rag and the broom and started cleaning up, figuring it'd maybe settle my mind."

"Did it?"

"Not so's you could notice," Burke said flatly, glancing at the door. "I got to thinking of the things I have to do, like picking up a hasp and padlock from Wolcott's tomorrow for that door, along with a window light."

"Better get a foot or so of chain and another padlock for that cell Whitman and his friend broke Rufe out of, too. Can't use the lock."

"Yeh. And talking about Rufe again, I just don't feel right about that, Marshal. I keep thinking I ought to own up to what I done, stand on my own feet, instead of letting you take the blame."

Rye shrugged. "Suits me, deputy. A few more men looking for the chance to even a score with me won't matter—the line's already too long to count. But you better be sure you can use that weapon you're packing, and use it good when Rufe's pals come looking for you to square up. They've already started, too. Whitman was the first, and there's that jasper who was with him, and got away from me. They won't be the only ones. Can bet at least a half a dozen more will remember real sudden that Rufe Custer was a friend of theirs, and take it on themselves to even the score. That's the way it always works."

Burke had turned, placed the broom in a corner. Taking the dust rag he'd been using from a pocket, he began to wipe the desk again.

"I'd be a damn fool to think I can stand up to that crowd."

"You're being smart. Admitting something like that to yourself takes sand, but it's the best thing to do. Let it stand the way it is—I'll handle it. I'm used to doing it."

Burke paused to consider the marshal's words. Finally he nodded. "Sure, you're right . . . you turn up anything on that army wagon you was telling me about?"

"No, asked around about it, too. Nobody seems to have seen it pass by. Aim to go back out there tomorrow if I get the chance, have myself a good look around, see if I can come up with something that'll give me an idea who was in on the ambush. Didn't have time today. That shooting at the Kansas City—Rufe killing that gambler—happened just as I was starting."

"Be glad to go along with you," Burke said. "Ain't been out that way in quite a spell." Leaning toward one of the benches, he picked up the sack containing the belongings of the dead soldiers and the report Rye had written of the incident.

"This ready to put on the stage in the morning for Fort Union?"

"Yes. Tell the driver to turn it over personally to the post commander, whoever he is."

"I ain't sure who's bossing them yellowlegs right now, there being some changes, I hear, but that jehu'll know. I'll make it real plain to him that—"

The deputy's voice faded as he saw Rye staring off into the north through the window. A deep frown knotted the marshal's features.

"Something wrong?"

"Looks like a fire—other side of town."

Burke stepped quickly to Rye's side. "Sure does," he said, and drew back slightly. "Marshal, about the only thing out there big enough to make a fire that size is the Montgomery place. You happen to name it when you was doing your asking around?"

Rye's mouth was set to a hard line. "Not once. Was careful, in fact, not to." Seizing the shotgun, he started for the door.

"Then I'm betting whoever put that wagon in the Montgomery barn heard you asking about it, and made tracks to set it a'fire. Means there was something there they sure didn't want you to find."

Rye only nodded as he hurried on. That assumption had come to him immediately, and another truth was now plain: the men, or at least one of them, who had been in on the ambush and murder of the soldiers from Fort Churchill, and the theft of the new double eagles, were right there in Crisscross!

Both the house and the barn were blazing furiously when Rye and Aaron Burke reached the Montgomery place. The mules were gone, probably running loose in the low hills, and a dozen or so men were busily involved —not in trying to put out the roaring blaze, but in keeping the flames from igniting the dry prairie grass and starting a range fire.

It was evident the conflagration had been started deliberately. The rank smell of coal oil was still heavy in the smoke-filled air, and that fact further convinced Rye that at least one of the outlaws involved in the ambush was in the settlement.

"Guess this puts the kibosh on your having a good look around here tomorrow," Burke said as they started back for town a time later.

Both were soot-streaked and sweaty from their labor at controlling the fires, as were the other men, mostly all cowhands who had noted the flames while en route to Crisscross and stopped to help. Rye, taking notice during the activities, recognized none of the town's merchants. It was likely, as the deputy remarked, that all were inside their establishments and thus were unable to see the glow of the fire.

Rye had little to say to that, or anything else as they returned to the jail, his thoughts being centered on the fire and its undeniable meaning. It was clear that one or more of the killers had been in the Palo Duro, or perhaps it was the Kansas City or the Parisian, when he asked about the army wagon. Since he had not mentioned where the vehicle was, only whoever had hidden it in the Montgomery barn would know to go there and take measures to destroy it.

Rye swore angrily to himself. He had been close, apparently, to finding out who the killers were, but had bungled it. Now whoever they were would be on guard, and there'd be little if any chance of them tipping their hand and betraying an identity. But there was no point in hashing it over; the army detail, when it arrived, would have to start from scratch.

"Be obliged to you if you'll see about those signs," he

said to Burke, getting his mind back on his own duties. "Pretty late, I know, but I want to get them up."

The deputy, halted with him beside the pump and trough behind the jail to wash up, nodded.

"Sure do my dangdest," he said, drying his face with his bandanna as he turned away. "I best hustle right along. . . . G'night."

"Good night," Rye replied, finishing up, and moving toward his quarters.

CHAPTER 14

Mada Fremont sat on the edge of the bed in John Rye's house. She listened to the lawman and old Aaron Burke, who had suddenly become a deputy sheriff again, converse as they stopped at the pump in the yard to wash up.

Dressed in her most revealing gown, a pink satin with much lace, she had been waiting for well over an hour for him to come. But it hadn't been too bad. There in the soft darkness and relative coolness of the lawman's quarters, it had been pleasant—a far cry from the noise, lamplight and rank odors that were prevalent in the Palo Duro.

But Mada supposed she shouldn't complain. Ben Delano, taking a fancy to her, had plucked her out of a St. Louis waterfront bordello and outfitted her with fine clothes. With the help of a madame who ran one of the fine "gentlemen's retreats," as they were called, he had given her an intensive course on the rudiments of being—or appearing to be—a lady. When he was satisfied she was ready, he took her with him as his shill on the riverboats, where his dexterity and honesty kept him in constant demand.

Ben was as straight as one in his profession was expected to be, and within three years he had built up a stake of nearly ten thousand dollars. But he was tiring of the river, and when he was approached by Vic Lefore, who had been run out of New Orleans by the police, to go in with him on a saloon and gambling house in a town called Crisscross, somewhere in New Mexico Territory, he had agreed.

Ben had given her a choice—take a thousand dollars and go her own way, or stick with him in this new venture and he'd cut her in on the profits. Naturally she chose the latter; she had no wish to return to St. Louis, or even open a place of her own. Being Ben Delano's woman and enjoying all the advantages that went with it was a hell of a lot better deal, and besides, she'd be in for a piece of the take, being a sort of partner.

An arrangement with Vic Lefore didn't work out for Ben, however, and shortly after they had arrived in Crisscross the two men split over just what sort of place their combined efforts should produce. Ben was for a high-toned gambling house and saloon, Lefore favored one where women would be the main draw.

As a result of that difference of opinion, and likes and dislikes, the partnership died aborning, and the two men went their separate ways—Lefore buying a saloon and renaming it the Parisian after sending for a dozen or so of the women who had worked for him in New Orleans.

Ben had sought to purchase a place down in the center of the settlement, which being at a crossroads was a popular stopover for cowboys, trail drivers and pilgrims alike, but the owner of the saloon, called the Bonanza, had refused to sell. Ben ended up buying another place, upon which he then spent most of his cash remodeling and enlarging.

When it was all done, the Palo Duro was as fine as any saloon west of the Missouri, Mada had heard it said, and she guessed it was. But Ben was dissatisfied with the take; there were so many saloons operating in Crisscross that business was diluted to a point he felt was far from satisfactory.

That was when he hit on the idea of taking over the town—not alone, but in combination with Lefore, Phil Reno and one each of the other merchants—all carefully chosen. It was nothing new, Ben had explained that night when those selected to form the combine, as he first termed it, gathered in a back room of the Palo Duro. Only a couple of years back, he pointed out, two brothers and several friends had taken over a town up in Kansas—Ellsworth Mada thought the name of it was—and ran it to suit themselves. He had mentioned other settlements, too.

It worked well, and within a year all competition as well as the bluenoses who had opposed Ben and the others were gone. It was a good setup, and the members of the council all prospered. The only problems they ever had were with lawmen, and that was solved by buying them off, or getting rid of them by some other more drastic means.

But now a definite shadow had fallen across the idyllic partnership. A different sort of lawman, one that even Ben seemed to respect and fear, had come to take over the town—a man who went by the name of John Rye. He also bore the somewhat ridiculous byname of the Doomsday Marshal, and he was said to be a hard-nosed, utterly dangerous man.

The lawman had fairly well demonstrated the truth of that already, in that he'd shot down three men, but he'd not be dealing with a Cahoon or a Rufe Custer or a Sam Whitman when he came up against her. She had never failed yet to win a man over to her way of thinking, and—

Mada's musings came to a stop. Rye and the deputy had finished whatever they were doing, and Burke was now taking his leave. Shortly afterward she heard the marshal's step in the doorway and listened as he entered, swearing softly as he walked into a chair or some other item of furniture. Then she heard the scratch of a match, and the house suddenly became aglow with lamplight. Rising, she crossed to the bedroom doorway and framed herself in its rectangle.

The lawman's reaction was instantaneous. She was scarcely there when she found herself looking into the muzzle of his pistol. She drew back, startled, aware suddenly that she had never been so close to death. Lips compressed, breathing heavily, she watched his coiled shape relent, straighten, and the muscular hand gripping the weapon draw back, returning the pistol to its holster.

"Lady," he said quietly, "you came within a frog's hair of getting yourself killed."

Mada's self-assurance was returning quickly. "Oh, I don't know, Marshal," she said, airily, "you wouldn't shoot a woman, would you?"

"Only if I had to," he replied, "and how in the hell would I know it was a woman at a time like this—showing up out of the dark unexpected?"

Mada crossed to a chair at the small table and sat down. She smiled coyly. "Now, Marshal, how many gunfighters and outlaws have you ever known that wore a pink dress and smell like I do?"

The question brought a half smile to Rye's lips. "Can't think of a one," he admitted. "Want to tell me what you're doing here?"

Mada returned his smile with one of her own, a pleasant display of even white teeth set between full, perfect
lips.

"I thought you might like a little company your first
night in town."

Rye, taking the chair opposite the woman, considered
her coolly. He would be considered better than good-
looking, Mada decided, if his mouth didn't have such a
grim set, and his eyes, a sort of gray-blue, weren't so pen-
etrating. They seemed to look right through a person.

"That straight—or did Delano and his friends send
you?"

Mada struggled to maintain an even expression. Rye
hadn't been fooled at all—and he believed in getting right
to the point. But at such disconcerting moments, she'd
learned long ago, it was smart to play it honest.

"I guess that is part of it, but mostly I wanted to really
meet you," she said, toying with the lace on the front of
her dress. "I've always had a hankering to meet famous
men, and I guess you're about as big and famous as they
get."

"The livery stable is full of that stuff," Rye said
indifferently. "Now, I'm needing sleep. Speak up if
you've got something to say."

"I've told you—I wanted to see you alone, meet you."

Rye shrugged, glanced toward the open door. The
night was quiet, the harsh clicking of a cricket somewhere
in the house and the distant hoot of an owl being the only
sounds.

"Why did you become a lawman?" Mada asked. She'd
not be brushed off, rushed by his seeming impatience.

She'd just go along, do things his way, gradually lead up to the business at hand.

"Good a job as any," he said, the square line of his wide shoulders stirring. "Like a man once said, somebody's got to pick the cotton."

Mada laughed, one of her best attributes, she knew. "Seems a terribly dangerous way to live, and I doubt if you make much money doing it."

"Maybe not. Never gave it much thought."

"Wouldn't you like to have a lot of money—enough to go somewhere, settle down and become a rancher, or go into a business of some kind?"

"No, can't say that I would."

"But don't you like the idea of plenty of money, hard cash?" Mada pressed, frowning.

"That what brings you here—you want to buy me off—get me to leave town?" he asked bluntly.

Mada felt something tighten within here. She was getting nowhere with John Rye, the first and only man she'd not been able to bend to her will. But she wasn't through yet.

"All right, I'll put my cards on the table," she said briskly. "Ben Delano and the others want you out, and they're willing to pay. Just name your price."

Rye considered her dispassionately. Rising, he stepped to the doorway, took up the shotgun he'd stood against the nearby wall and put it inside the bedroom. Mada followed him.

"There's no price. I'm not for sale."

Anger flashed through her. "You're a fool!" she cried. "Can't you see you're being given a choice—a lot of cash money, or ending up in the brakes like the lawmen before you?"

Rye shrugged, said, "Sure—"

Mada's anger rose even higher. The man's attitude was infuriating! Stepping back, she started for the doorway.

"You're a fool, John Rye, a plain damn fool!"

The lawman's brows lifted in mock dismay. "This mean you're leaving? I thought you aimed to keep me company for the night. Was looking forward to it!"

Mada paused in the opening, gave him a withering glance over a slim shoulder. She had failed completely, utterly—and it was hard to swallow.

"Oh, go to hell!" she snapped, and hurried off into the night.

CHAPTER 15

John Rye was up early that next morning, but Aaron Burke was in the office ahead of him. The signs forbidding the carrying of guns in the town were there, placed along the wall, the paint still a bit wet.

"Just what we need," Rye said, standing the shotgun in the wall rack. "Your friend did a good job."

"It's going to cost an extra five dollars 'cause he had to work most all night getting them made."

"Worth it," Rye said. "Find out how much we owe him, and I'll pay. Had your breakfast?"

The deputy nodded. "A hour ago. You want me to start putting up them signs?"

"Like for you to take the two big ones that go at each end of the street. Nail them to a tree or post, something good and solid, where they'll be seen easy by riders coming in."

Burke nodded, turned to one of the benches and picked up a hammer and a can of nails he had apparently brought with him from his home. "What about the others?"

"I'll take care of them—want to be there to handle any objections. There another hammer around here? And I'll need some of those nails."

"There's a hand ax out back," the deputy replied, surrendering some of the nails to the marshal. "I'll fetch it."

Burke hurried down the hall fronting the cells and disappeared into the yard behind the jail, returning shortly with the implement, called a kindling hatchet by some.

"That'll do fine," Rye said, thrusting the handle of the small ax under his belt as he might a spare pistol. He dropped a few of the nails into a vest pocket, collected the three smaller signs and started for the doorway. Burke followed slowly, his lean face a dark study.

"Something bothering you?" Rye asked, taking note.

"I'm sort of wondering about these here signs. Some of them jaspers ain't going to take kindly to forking over their hardware."

"Tough," Rye said laconically. "It's the law, and they'll obey it or answer to me."

"But it ain't really the law. There ain't no—"

"They don't know that, and if they've been around the country much they will have run into the same rule in plenty of towns."

Burke shrugged. "Sure do hope it works."

"It will—fact is, it's up to us to make it work," the marshal said, and moved off up the deserted street.

The town was quiet at that early hour, and with the heat yet to come it was a pleasant time. Meadowlarks were whistling in the fields near the church, and ducks were quacking busily on the creek. Crisscross had probably been a fine place to live before the alliance of greedy merchants had taken over, Rye thought, and it would be again if things worked out right.

The Palo Duro was the first saloon along the street. As he passed the general store, which stood between the jail and Delano's place, Rye saw Frank Wolcott in the door-

way of his establishment watching him intently. The lawman nodded, held up the signs in a way that allowed the
store owner to read the lettering and continued on his
way, not waiting to assess Wolcott's reaction.

The Palo Duro was open, but only a bartender and two
swampers were in the building. All came out onto the
porch when they heard the sound of the edict being
nailed alongside the door. It was the bartender who spoke
up.

"Ain't sure Mr. Delano's going to like this. Fact is, I'm
damn sure ain't nobody going to cotton to it."

"It's a new law," Rye said coldly, "and they better like
it. And I want this sign left up, understand? If there's
somebody wants to talk about it, tell them to come see
me."

"What'll I do if some of them come in packing guns?"

"Tell them they'd better leave them at the bar with
you, otherwise they'll find themselves in my jail."

The bartender nodded, shrugged. "Sure, Marshal, just
what I'll do."

The lawman moved on to the Kansas City, next on that
side of the street. The door was shut, and his hammering
brought no one to investigate the cause. At the Parisian,
on the opposite side, he again drew objection—this time
from three cowboys who had evidently spent the night
and were returning to their jobs.

"You figure you can make that there rule stick?" one, a
squat, leather-faced man with bloodshot eyes asked.

"Aim to."

There was a pause, and then one of the others said,
"Well, I sure wouldn't want your job of trying to. I've
seen a few gun sharks hanging around here that don't

shuck their hoglegs even when they crawl into their soogans."

Rye smiled tightly. "It's going to be different around here from now on—remember that. Next time you come, leave your guns in your saddlebags or hand them over to the bartender."

The squat one turned his head, spat into the dust. "*If* we come back," he said. "This here town was a place where a man could have hisself a whooping good time without nobody hollering whoa. I reckon that ain't how it's going to be from now on."

The marshal shook his head. "You can still raise all the hell you want as long as you don't use a gun, and stay inside."

The trio of riders considered that briefly, and then turning, stepped down off the Parisian's porch. Spurs jingling, they headed for their horses waiting hipshot at the hitchrack.

Rye, the chore of erecting the signs finished, stood for a long minute in front of the saloon, then finally moved off along the walk, retracing his steps back down the street. He guessed he could have his breakfast now, after which he'd drop by the livery stable for a talk with Jeremiah Potter, see if the man could furnish information on the army wagon, now only bits of charred wood, ashes and twisted metal.

Who could have set the Montgomery place on fire? He had probed his mind several times during the night when, sleepless, he lay mulling it about in his head. If he could just recall a marked reaction on the part of someone while he was voicing his questions in the saloon, he would have the answer. But he could come up with nothing.

His thoughts swung to Mada Fremont and her visit to his quarters. He wondered if there had been some connection between her being there, supposedly to keep him occupied while a torch was being put to the Montgomery place. If true, it would mean Ben Delano was involved in the murders and theft.

He discarded the idea as unlikely. Mada had apparently been waiting for some time in his house, and if it had been her intention to keep him busy while the fire was being set, she undoubtedly would have made her presence known earlier.

Rye swore softly. He was finding it difficult to keep his mind on the task that faced him in Crisscross. His thoughts continually returned to the question of who had ambushed the soldiers and gotten away with a chest filled with two hundred thousand dollars in gold double eagles. He supposed if he hadn't come upon the wheel prints, and subsequently the wagon itself, the matter would not press too heavily on his conscience. It was the fact that the killers had gone to Crisscross after the murders and theft to strip and abandon the wagon—and logically were still in the settlement—that kept digging at his mind.

Rye hesitated as Burke approached, pointing for the other end of the street to erect his second sign. He'd had to provide a post for the first one, the deputy explained, which accounted for his taking so much time. The marshal assured him that a few more minutes didn't matter. Advising the deputy where he would be, he walked slowly on toward the Bluebird.

He had the sudden, intuitive feeling that he was being watched, and glancing about saw Wolcott, this time with another man whose features were not identifiable, again standing in his doorway. There was also a small crowd in front of the Kansas City now, and in two of the second floor windows of the Parisian he could see faces. The no-gun signs were drawing attention, he reckoned.

Reaching the Bluebird, Rye pulled back the door. Entering, he settled himself at a side table where he would have a view of the street. He was the only patron, probably the first of the day, and when Mueller himself approached to take his order—one for steak, eggs, biscuits and coffee—Rye found himself being served quickly. Giving that thought as he began to eat, the lawman wondered if such was accountable to his being the first and only customer, or did Herman Mueller want to get him out of his place of business as fast as possible.

Mueller offered no conversation, but returned to the sanctuary of his kitchen immediately, and Rye fell to enjoying the good food. A short time later he saw Burke arrive at the jail carrying a pane of glass for the broken window and a small sack that evidently contained the hasp and other articles that were needed to make repairs.

Three riders passed by heading for one of the saloons. All were tough-looking, hardcase individuals wearing full-length yellow dusters and hats pulled low over their faces. They gave Burke, working at replacing the window light, a thorough going-over with their eyes as they passed.

Just before Rye finished the meal, the southbound stage swept into town in a whirl of dust, and Burke, obtaining the sack destined for the commander at Fort Union, carried it to where the coach had halted in front of the general store. Rye watched the deputy toss the sack up to the driver and engage him in conversation during which he probably relayed instructions given him as to the delivery of the sack. Then, coming about, Burke returned to the jail where he resumed his labors.

Having Aaron turn up as his deputy was a stroke of good luck, the lawman thought as he pushed back his chair and prepared to leave. Not only was he well acquainted with the town and its people and problems, but he was a handy man with tools as well.

At the scrape of Rye's chair legs on the bare floor, Mueller reappeared, and hurried to the table, a small pot in his big hand.

"More coffee, Marshal?"

Rye shook his head. "How much do I owe you?"

"Seventy-five cents."

The lawman selected the necessary coins from those in his pocket, handed them over without comment and started to turn away.

"Marshal—"

At the restaurant man's voice, Rye halted. "Yeh?"

"The signs you have nailed up. I could not read them so good when you and the deputy came from the jail, but do they say that a man cannot carry his pistol?"

The lawman nodded. "Pistol, rifle or shotgun. I don't want anybody walking around the town carrying a firearm."

Mueller sighed deeply. "It will mean much trouble, for all of us. I hope you—"

"Don't worry about it," the lawman cut in curtly. "I know what I'm doing," he added, and continued on to the door.

Pushing open the dust-clogged screen, Rye stepped out onto the walk. The stage rolled by, gathering speed in a newly spun cloud of tan. The lawman hesitated until the pall had drifted on, then recalled his intentions to speak with Potter at the livery stable. He turned left and began a long tangent for the sprawling structure.

In that next instant the sharp crack of a pistol shattered the quiet that had temporarily claimed the town, and John Rye recoiled as a bullet ripped through the fabric of his sleeve.

The lawman reacted instinctively and instantaneously. Spinning, he lunged to one side, pivoted again and threw himself into the doorway of the vacant building standing a few steps from the Bluebird Restaurant.

The sniper was in the weedy lot that lay between Wolcott's General Store and the Palo Duro. From the corner of an eye the marshal caught the puff of smoke blossoming at the side of the sagging old shack that was near center of the open ground.

There was movement directly across the street as Aaron Burke, shotgun in hand, appeared in the doorway, his narrow face betraying the anxiety he felt. He stared questioningly at the marshal, who shook his head to signify that he had not been hurt, and then waved the deputy back.

Taut, Rye put his attention again on the old shack. His best chance was to drop back behind the empty building he was in, staying in the area in the rear of the Bluebird and the other structures on that side of the street, until he reached Nate Stout's place. The gun and saddle shop was more or less directly opposite from where the bushwhacker had fired his bullet. Like as not, the man would have moved by the time Stout's was reached. But there was the possibility that luck would be with him, the marshal figured, and he'd get a glimpse of whoever it was.

Sam Whitman's partner had gone running off into the night that first time an attempt was made to cut him down, and this could be the killer trying again to get the job done. Or it could be some outlaw enraged over the no-gun order, seeking to put an end to the regulation by ridding the town of the man who instigated it.

Moving hurriedly, John Rye crossed behind the Bluebird, old Bonanza standing bleak and hollow in the now warming sunlight, and reached the near side of the deserted structure next to Stout's. Moving to the back door, he found it nailed shut. Muttering a curse, he continued on to the corner of the building, bent low, and threw his glance across to the shack where he had seen the puff of smoke. There was no one to be seen, but he kept his gaze on the area, letting his eyes switch back and forth from the rear of the Palo Duro and Wolcott's store while encompassing the lot in between.

There were no signs of movement anywhere within his range of vision. Pistol in hand, fully alert for any motion and sound, Rye made his way along the wall of the building until he reached the forward corner that faced the street.

The gunshot had drawn attention. Several men were on the porch of the Palo Duro, and that of the Kansas City. The Parisian had been aroused also, and he could see Vic Lefore with two men and several women—one of them the little dark French girl, Renee. Rye was unable to see if Stout was at his window, that view being blocked by the building itself, but Frank Wolcott had come out on the store's landing and was looking about trying to determine where the shot had come from.

It was useless to remain where he was. He was gaining nothing, and while he stalled the would-be assassin could be slipping away. Pivoting, Rye returned to the alley and crossed behind Stout's and the Parisian. Halting at the big, spreading cottonwood overshadowing the hitching rack at its side long enough to get his breath, he spurted for the opposite side of the street.

Without slowing, he ran through the lot between Delano's place and Reno's Kansas City Saloon to the alley back of them. Rushing on, weapon ready, he continued to the far rear corner of the Palo Duro before he drew up. From that point of vantage he had a clear look at the shack and the lot where the bushwhacker was hiding.

Again there was no indication of anyone being there, unless the sniper was hiding inside the old shack. Grim set, breathing hard, cursing softly at what he knew must be done, Rye hunched low and made a run for the sagging structure, zigzagging from side to side so as to offer no easy target.

He gained the shed with no challenging gunfire from its interior, and crowded up close to its rear wall. Sweating freely now from his efforts, he raised himself slightly and peered into the glassless window. Again he swore. There was no one inside.

But whoever was out to kill him was somewhere along the street—that was certain. There had been no quick pound of hoofs which would indicate the bushwhacker had mounted his horse and hurried off. The town lay in complete silence while those within it watched with interest—most, no doubt, with fervent hope that the next bullet directed at him would not miss.

Moving to the front of the shack, the marshal sent his glance along the street. There was no one to be seen in the open, only Nate Stout in the doorway of his store opposite. Rye caught the man's eye and held his attention for a long minute, thinking Stout might have seen where the bushwhacker had gone and would betray it by some unconscious sign or action.

But Stout, if he knew, remained motionless, and Rye turned his attention elsewhere. The merchant would have been careful to withhold any possible tip-off anyway. Like everyone else in the damned town—except Aaron Burke—Stout would like to see him dead.

The lawman's glance halted on the group in front of the Parisian. Renee, he noted, had moved a bit to one side, and was now standing at the corner of the saloon. When she saw that he was looking at her, the woman turned slightly, and arm partly hidden from the others, pointed in the direction of the buildings on the same—the east—side of the street.

Rye caught it immediately. The bushwhacker had crossed over, probably while he was circling to get in behind him, and was now holed up in one of the old, vacant structures—but which? There were several, chief among them being the one that had previously housed the Bonanza. Being the largest in the row, and containing several rooms, it was the most logical.

"Marshal! Marshal!"

The urgent, hoarse whisper came from a pile of crates and boxes behind the general store. It was Aaron Burke.

"That building the Bonanza was in—I seen him duck in there. You want me to—"

"Stay put in the office," Rye answered. "I'll handle him."

Abruptly he turned away. The French girl had been doing him a favor, despite the fact they were on opposite sides, and he owed her a favor. Rye studied the weathered structure, once a fine saloon. The door in the front was open, and the glass in all of the windows had been broken, but it did have a blind side—from the north.

The marshal delayed no more. Pivoting, he dropped back to the alley, continued along it until he was beyond the Palo Duro where a fairly large crowd of onlookers had gathered on the porch. Ignoring them, he recrossed the street.

He knew that he must move fast; the outlaw in the Bonanza would not wait for him, particularly if he had caught sight of him as he doubled back. Wasting no time, but throwing an appreciative smile at Renee as he passed, the lawman reached the alley lying to the east of that row of buildings, and hurriedly made it to the rear of the abandoned saloon.

The door stood ajar, half off its hinges. Relying on a hunch that the killer did not expect him to appear so soon, the lawman stepped quickly inside the hushed, musty building and glanced about its gloomy interior. He was in what had been the main part of the saloon. Two doors over on his left indicated separate rooms used for some purpose. Moving silently, Rye started for the first. A man hiding out while keeping an eye on the street would likely choose such quarters.

John Rye had guessed wrong in that. Midway along the

wall a figure rose suddenly from behind a pile of trash and other debris just inside the door. The lawman saw the dull, metallic glint in the man's hand and fired instantly. The bushwhacker stiffened, threw up his arms, staggered back and fell through the open doorway, half in, half out of the building.

Rye, motionless as the echoes of the gunshot rocked back and forth in the old building and coils of powder smoke drifted lazily about him, finally stirred. Raising his weapon, he removed the spent cartridge and reloaded. Then, moving forward, he crossed to the Bonanza's entrance, stepped over the fallen gunman and came out onto the walk.

He could hear people hurrying up from the direction of the saloons. Coming from across the street was Aaron Burke, carrying the shotgun, approaching at a run.

"He dead?" the deputy asked, crouching beside the man and feeling for a pulse. "Deader than a doornail," he added, answering his own question as he straightened up. "He the jasper that was with Sam Whitman last night?"

Rye shook his head. "No, don't think so. This fellow's tall, skinny. Man last night looked short and a bit heavy." Raising his glance, the lawman swept the gathering crowd. "Any of you know him?"

One of the riders said, "Seen him last night, don't know him."

"Where'd you see him?"

"The Palo Duro. Was talking to that fellow who owns it—Ben. Heard him say he was riding through."

A drifter, according to that—and judging from his appearance. Suspicion rose swiftly within Rye. Delano had failed to get anywhere in sending Mada Fremont to buy him off; had he then hired this man to kill him? The law-man moved to the edge of the walk, glanced about for the saloon keeper. Delano was standing in front of the gun and saddle shop, talking to Stout. Moving purposefully up the street, Rye confronted him.

"When that woman of yours couldn't swing me over last night, did you hire that drifter to put a bullet in me?" he demanded harshly.

Delano smiled coolly and shook his head. "You're bark-ing up the wrong tree, Marshal."

Rye's smoldering anger did not lessen. "Maybe—and maybe not. You were talking to him last night."

"I talk to a lot of men, some of them drifters," Delano said, unperturbed. "Want to know something, Marshal? I was just telling Nate here that you've just about killed more men in this town in less than two days than's been done in two years."

"That ought to mean something to you," Stout added, "and if you're half as smart as folks think you are, you'll see that you're making things bad around here, doing all this killing! And them no-gun signs you've put up—they're sure going to cause trouble!"

Rye was silent as a murmur of agreement from men standing nearby reached him. He'd been forced to kill three times—four counting Rufe Custer for whom he'd taken the blame—and in all cases he'd had no choice. But that was to be expected; just as you had to catch a horse before you could ride him, there would be shootings in a wild town like Crisscross before the law could gain con-trol. He was tempted to point out that truth, but he let it pass, just as he had dismissed the opportunity to ask about the burning of the old Montgomery place.

At the moment he was more interested in knowing who had hired the drifter to kill him, but he supposed that was something he'd likely never know since the would-be killer was dead and in no condition to talk, and his employer would certainly never admit being a party to the attempt. It could have been one of the council members anxious to rid himself of the threat to his prosperity, or perhaps it was one of the hardcases packing a grudge and unwilling to undertake the chore of cutting Rye down himself. Hell, the probabilities were limitless!

Turning away, Rye nodded to Burke, and together they started for the sheriff's office. Reaching it, the marshal swung his eyes again to the old Bonanza building and the crowd still gathered in front of it. Potter was there now, had laid out his stretcher, and with the aid of a bystander was placing the drifter's body on it. Close by, three men—cowhands or drovers with a trail drive judging from the worn, weather-faded condition of their clothing—were entering the Bluebird in quest of a meal.

"Somebody hired that jasper to go gunning for me," Rye said, his voice still tight with anger. "Sure like to know who it was."

"Expect I could do some guessing, and come close," Burke said, and moved to the window. Brushing at the sweat on his face, he swore softly.

"Looks like more trouble, Marshal," he said. "That Mex gunfighter—the one they call Tascosa—he's coming down the street, and he's got one of them signs in his hand."

CHAPTER 16

Rye followed the deputy's glance. A squat, swarthy man wearing two pistols in crossed belts was approaching. Dressed in customary *vaquero* style, he had pushed his large, rolled-brim hat off his head and was allowing it to hang by the chin string on his back. In his left hand was one of the signs that had been posted at the entrance to a saloon; with the right he was waving to onlookers along the street who were cheering him on. A round dozen or so men trailed the gunman, who was making a big show of his advance.

Rye, in no mood at that moment to brook opposition of any sort, waited until the Mexican had drawn abreast of the jail, and then abruptly stepped out onto the landing.

The *vaquero* came to a rocking, unsteady halt at the lawman's sudden appearance, and the shouts of approval and encouragement directed to him died as quickly.

Rye, eyes narrowed, nodded coldly. "Something on your mind?" he asked in a brittle voice.

Tascosa, recovering somewhat, grinned broadly, his large white teeth contrasting sharply with his dark skin.

"Sí, *jefe*, this damn sign," he replied, throwing the piece of lettered wood at the lawman's feet. "For no man do I not wear my pistols."

Rye bent forward, picked up the sign. His features

were set, completely devoid of expression, and his voice was low and controlled. "You're going to take them off if you hang around this town. It's the law."

"No, my friend, this I cannot do. My *pistolas* are a part of me, as my arms, my hands. I wear them even when I go to bed."

There was laughter at the *vaquero's* remark, and he turned to smile appreciatively at his audience. The marshal waited until the merriment had ceased, then moved closer to the man.

"If that's how you want it, then mount up and ride out. Here you go by the law, or move on."

A mutter of protest came from the bystanders. Farther up the street, near the saloons, a second crowd had gathered and were watching the confrontation from the distance.

Tascosa swiped at his glistening face with the back of a hand. "No, *jefe*, I do not surrender my guns, and I do not leave. Here I will stay, and will fight you if—"

Rye's pistol was out and leveled at the *vaquero* before he could finish the sentence. Stepping in closer, the lawman jammed the muzzle of his weapon into the man's belly. Tascosa hurriedly raised his hands.

"Maybe," Rye said softly, "but first you got a little job to do. Turn around."

Tascosa pivoted slowly, the silver trimmings on his pants and vest glittering in the sunlight as he moved. The crowd began to part, pull away.

"Walk!" Rye directed, pressing the barrel of his pistol into the man's spine. "You're going to put this sign back up, then you'll have a choice—get on your horse and ride out, or try your luck using one of those fancy six-shooters on me."

Tascosa made no reply. No longer smiling, he headed back up the street. The lawman, ignoring the scattered crowd, now drawn well away and allowing him and the *vaquero* ample room to pass, glanced back. A tight smile pulled at his mouth and he nodded slightly in approval. Aaron Burke, the shotgun cradled in his arms, was bringing up the rear a dozen paces behind.

The Palo Duro sign was still in place, Rye saw as they drew near. The one at the Parisian had not been removed either, which left only the Kansas City. Passing in front of Delano's, the marshal gave the people gathered there a brief look and prodded the *vaquero* firmly, keeping him moving until they had reached the last saloon. Drawing a bit to one side of the man, Rye handed him the sign.

"Put it back up. Can use the butt of your pistol for a hammer."

The Mexican did as he was ordered. Holding the sign in place with one hand and carefully drawing one of his pistols with the other, he began to hammer the nails back into the wood near the doorway. Shortly Phil Reno appeared, but he said nothing, simply watched in angry silence.

When the sign was in place, Rye jerked a thumb at the horses standing along the nearby hitchrack.

"Now, get out!" he said tersely.

"Damn it—you can't do that!" Reno shouted, coming forward. "You ain't got no right running my business off, and I just ain't going to put up with it—none of us are!"

The marshal, pistol still in his hand, ignored the saloon

keeper while he continued to center his close attention on Tascosa, now walking slowly toward the horses.

"Don't get any foolish ideas, *amigo*," Rye warned quietly. "Make a move to draw on me, and I'll kill you."

The *vaquero* did not reply. Coming to the rack, he stepped in beside his horse, a fine-looking palomino. Yanking the reins free, Tascosa swung up into the heavy, ornate saddle. Turning, he glanced back at Reno.

"This no is a good place to come now," he said in a matter-of-fact way, and cutting the big, honey-colored gelding about, struck off up the road leading from town at a brisk trot.

"This here's got to stop!" Reno shouted, facing Rye. "You're—you're plain ruining things for us!"

Rye shrugged, holstered his weapon. "Not what I want to do—I'm just here to see that the law is upheld. Now if that don't set with some of your customers—tough." The lawman paused, faced the crowd. Burke had pulled off to one side, the shotgun in the crook of his left arm now. An expression of confidence covered his features.

"I'll tell you all again," Rye continued in a strong voice. "The law's here to stay—you better get that in your heads. Long as it's obeyed, I'll give you no trouble. Break it and you'll answer to—"

"A bullet—that how you'll handle it?" a familiar, sarcastic voice asked from the crowd. "Killing seems to be your answer to everything."

Rye settled his cold gaze on the speaker. It was Wolcott. "If that's what it takes. I make a habit of giving a man a choice, however."

"I figure we've got a choice," the general store owner said, coming forward and taking a stand beside Phil

Reno. "This is our town. We built it, and we've got the right to tell you to move on."

"I'm agreeing with Frank!" Reno said loudly. "We're the ones—us men in business—who're getting hurt by your high-handed way of showing your authority—which we sure'n hell didn't give you!"

"I'm giving you something, though—right now," Wolcott said, "and I know I've got the backing of Phil, here, and Delano and Lefore—and everybody else in town! I'm ordering you once and for all to get the hell out—forget this law thing. We don't want it, and by God, we don't have to accept it!"

Rye's features were bleak as a Montana winter. "You're wrong, mister. You're going to get it whether you want it or not."

A silence followed the lawman's brittle words. It held for almost a minute, and then a man leaning against the corner post of the Palo Duro's porch straightened up and shrugged.

"Hell, I'd say we already got it," he declared in a voice filled with disgust. "Let's ride, boys—won't be nothing doing around here no more."

"You've got it wrong," Rye said. "You're welcome here, same as you are in any decent town, as long as you behave yourself. And that means no fighting in the street, no hurrahing the place—and leaving your gun in your saddlebag or with the bartender."

The cowboy considered, staring dully at the warped toes of his boots. Then, "Hell's fire, Marshal, you ain't leaving us no fun a'tall!"

"For sure," the man next to him confirmed. "It'll be

just like wearing hobbles! Things just ain't going to be the same around here."

"You can bank on that," Rye said flatly. Stepping down into the street, he headed for the jail with Aaron Burke walking at his side.

When they reached the jail, Rye glanced back. The crowd in front of the saloons was now larger than before, and among those who had joined it he spotted Delano, Vic Lefore and the two gunmen, Grissom and Turner. He could not locate, although it was difficult to distinguish many in the gathering, Nate Stout and Potter. And of course Herman Mueller—who, it appeared, seldom took any active part in the council's activities.

"I reckon they're making up their minds that we've for dang sure got law around here," Burke said, continuing on into the building. "You sure made that *vaquero* eat dirt!"

Rye's shoulders stirred. "Never like shaming any man, but sometimes it has to be done. Been intending to talk to Potter about that wagon and those mules. Maybe this'd be a good time."

"You want me keeping an eye on your back?" Burke said quickly.

"No, don't think it will be necessary. Obliged just the same."

"Proud to do it," the deputy said. Taking up his tools, he prepared to resume work on the repairs he was making.

Rye found Jeremiah Potter in the small office he maintained in one corner of the large, tin-roof building, already beginning to fill with heat. The stableman glanced up as he entered.

"Howdy, Marshal," he said, a noticeable lack of hostility in his manner. "Something I can do for you?"

"That fire last night—the Montgomery place—there was an army wagon in the barn, and four mules in the corral. Want to know if you saw the wagon when it went through, or past, town."

Potter shook his head. "Sure didn't. Heard you'd been asking about some wagon, but I can't help you none."

Rye pulled off his hat, brushed at his forehead. "Somebody around here's bound to have seen it. Tracks show it came in from the north, or northwest, circled that big hill west of town, and went on till it got to the Montgomery homestead where it was put in the barn."

"If it done all that at night, it ain't surprising that nobody seen it. Daytime maybe, but for sure not at night. Everybody's so damn busy in the saloons then that a cyclone could carry off the rest of the town and they'd never know it till next day."

The lawman studied Potter thoughtfully. The words had been spoken in jest, but he had detected an underlying note of bitterness.

"I can understand that," he said. "Still hard to believe nobody saw a rig as big as that one would have been when it went by. You know or hear anything about the mules? All army stock, branded U.S."

"Weren't brought here for damn sure." Potter's voice showed irritation. "Why? What do you keep digging at me for? This got something to do with the law here?"

"Not directly, but it is a law matter."

"Well, I sure ain't seen it."

"Somebody has," the marshal said quietly, replacing his hat and leaning back against the wall, which was well covered with calendars from feed companies and other concerns involved in the care of livestock. "Right after I asked around about it, somebody put a torch to the place and burnt it to the ground."

Potter's round face pulled into a frown as he scrubbed at the back of his neck. The fringes of his beard and mustache were discolored by tobacco juice.

"Way that looks, I'd say there was somebody in town that didn't want you poking into things out there."

"Just what I figure. Something else I'd like to ask you."

"Shoot—"

"Any of the merchants—the council—leave town for a day or two lately?"

Potter nodded immediately. "Yeh, Ben, and his lady friend, Mada Fremont. Went up to Colorado for a couple of days. They're figuring on opening up another saloon somewhere up there, Ben said."

"How long were they gone?"

Potter had to give that thought. "Like I said, it was a couple of days and nights—or maybe it was three, I ain't exactly sure. Why?"

"Just trying to fit some pieces together. Can you remember when that was?"

"About a week ago, more or less. Hell, Marshal, why don't you go talk to Delano about it? I plain don't like passing on something that just ain't none of my business."

Rye smiled. "Expect that's what I'll do, but I'm obliged to you."

"Welcome . . . seen what you done to that Mex, Tascosa, a bit ago."

The lawman drew himself upright. Here it came again: opposition to the measures he was being forced to take in establishing law and order in the settlement—the complaint that he was destroying business, that he had no right to—

"Was mighty pleased to see you doing that. And the way you're making some of them others toe the mark—it's a real good thing. Why, there ain't been nobody hurrahing the town since you got here!"

Rye stared at the stable owner. "You changing your mind? You're a member of the council, and wanted things to stay as they are."

"Yeh," Potter said, shrugging. He produced a plug of black tobacco from a pocket in his overalls; when the lawman refused a portion, he bit off a corner and stowed it away in the hollow of a cheek. "I reckon so, but I ain't so set on it now 'cause things ain't been all that good. I guess a man could say I've been getting my eyes opened."

A trickle of encouragement flowed through John Rye. Was resistance to law in Crisscross, like the mighty walls of Jericho, beginning to crumble?

"Meaning?" the lawman pressed.

"Well, maybe this idea of having business trimmed down to where we—the council members—don't have no competition is not all it's cracked up to be. I know this for dang sure, it ain't been no big help to me. We don't get pilgrims no more, and the folks that used to live here about most all have moved away, and them that's got places out on the flats and in the hills don't do their trading here no more—drive to Collinsville instead.

"When it comes right down to hard nails, I ain't doing even half the business I used to, and when you figure the damage them drunks and hells do when they're on a tear, it's costing me."

"Usually the way of it," Rye said. "You can't do business with that kind unless you got a lawman to keep them in line."

"That's for damn sure—I'm finally starting to realize it. It's only the saloons that're making good money. I don't think Wolcott and Nate Stout and the Dutchman are coming out any better'n me."

"Wolcott's done a lot of talking about wanting me to move on, leave things in town as they are. I guessed he was doing a big business."

Potter shifted the cud in his mouth, spat into a tin-bucket cuspidor placed in a corner. "Nah, Frank's just too dang proud to admit he's been wrong, I expect. Anyway, I'm glad you showed up, Marshal, and I'm gladder that you're getting some law back on the street."

"Trying—"

"Well, you're doing it! You're making it stick, and like I said, it's a real good thing and I'm glad of it. It'd be nice to see this town back like it was four, five years ago."

Rye moved for the door. The heat in the small, airless cubicle with its unshielded tin roof was intense, and he could feel sweat beginning to course down his body.

"There any of the others starting to see things the same as you do?"

Potter shook his head. "I ain't speaking for nobody but myself, and I'd take it as a favor if you'd keep all this between you and me—leastwise for a while. But I can do some feeling around, if you want."

"It would be a big help. I'd like to know who I can figure on if it all boils down to taking sides."

A frown knotted Jeremiah Potter's face. Again he shifted the wad of tobacco in his mouth, and spat a stream of brown juice into the bucket. "Well, now, Marshal," he said, nervously brushing at his mustache. "I ain't so sure that I—"

A half smile cracked the lawman's mouth. Potter's reaction was what could be expected, generally. All too often people wanted no part in enforcing the law, only the benefits derived from such.

"Was your idea—but forget it," Rye said. "If you get a chance to talk to Mueller and the other two you mentioned without getting yourself in a pickle, I'd like to know how they feel down deep."

"Sure, Marshal, I reckon I can do that much," Potter said as Rye moved through the doorway of the office, out into the runway and on to the street.

Reaching there, the lawman halted, taking a few moments to enjoy the slight breeze drifting in from the hills. Then, turning onto the board sidewalk, he began his return to the jail. He'd be pleased when the detail from Fort Union arrived to take over the matter of tracking down the outlaws who had ambushed the soldiers and stolen the gold. He had accomplished nothing other than getting the wagon, which might have furnished some clues, destroyed. Trying to do two jobs at the same time, and do them right, just wasn't possible.

But he reckoned he'd made some progress toward bringing law back to Crisscross and making it a decent town in which people could live. Outlaws, cowhands, drifters and the like, were beginning to understand that the wild, wide open town they had patronized was changing, that they had best find another place where they could pursue their violent, ungovernable ways.

It had been a pleasant surprise to hear Jeremiah Potter

express his satisfaction with the change, and state that he'd like to see things in Crisscross as they were before the council—which included himself—took over, and made of the town a closed settlement insofar as other merchants were concerned. From the way the stableman talked, there was also a good chance that Mueller, Stout and Frank Wolcott would eventually side with him.

Rye glanced ahead, aware that Aaron Burke, standing out in front of the jail, was anxiously beckoning to him. The lawman's mouth tightened. Something had gone wrong, he thought as he quickened his steps. Let a man ease off for a moment, pat himself on the back a little, and things started falling apart!

"Was about to come get you!" the deputy said in an excited voice as he moved aside for the lawman to enter his office. "This lady here's got something you're going to be mighty interested to see."

Rye smiled at Renee, the French girl from the Parisian. She was sitting on one of the benches, and appeared considerably disheveled, as if she had endured more than ordinary roughness at the hands of some customer. At her feet was a small carpetbag. It evidently contained all her belongings.

"Show the marshal what you got," Burke prompted as Renee returned Rye's greeting.

Opening the reticule she carried looped to her wrist, the woman withdrew a coin and handed it to the lawman. It was a shining new double eagle.

CHAPTER 17

A surge of elation rolled through John Rye. At last something definite to go on! He examined the gold piece closely. It could only be one of the stolen coins.

"The lady come here looking for help," he heard Burke explain. "Vic Lefore slapped her around right smart and throwed her out. Claimed she'd done something to help you when you was after that drifter."

Rye nodded. "Pointed out where he was hiding. I owe her a favor for that."

The deputy continued: "She's sort of scared to be around, and there won't be no stagecoach coming through for a week—"

"She can stay in my house," Rye said. "Won't anybody bother her there."

Renee smiled gratefully. One side of her face was beginning to discolor, and there was still a bit of blood in a corner of her mouth. Lefore, it seemed, was a big man when it came to working over his women, Rye thought; he'd bear that in mind and remember to accord the saloon keeper the same kind of treatment when and if the occasion presented itself—hopefully in the near future.

"Where did you get this double eagle?" he asked.

"Was asking her if she had enough money to get to the next town," Burke said before the woman could reply.

"She opened up that there pocketbook thing of hers and showed me what she had—and I spotted the double eagle. You figure it's one of them from that army shipment?"

"Sure of it," Rye replied, impatient to hear Renee's answer. Handing the coin back to her, he asked again, "Where did you get this? Can you remember who gave it to you?"

Renee's shoulders lifted, and fell. "Of course, monsieur, it was the man Grissom."

Will Grissom! He was the hired gun who looked after the merchants' interests, and took care of any of the town's patrons who got out of line. Rye recalled seeing him with Wolcott that previous night in the Parisian, and again that morning on the street.

"It was when I tell him I want my money," Renee explained. "He had gambled, lost all but this twenty dollars. He tell me to wait but I get angry so he gave the gold to me but said I was to only keep it for him until he could bring me silver. It was a good luck charm."

"Not for him," Rye murmured. "When was this?"

"This morning—early."

The explanation was clear. Grissom knew it would be dangerous to spend any of the stolen gold, but had let Renee have the double eagle to keep her quiet—with instructions to hang on to it until he could get ordinary money to replace it.

"He tell you when he'd be back after the—after his good luck charm?"

Again the woman shrugged. "No—tonight perhaps, or maybe sooner. It does no longer matter. He will not know where to look for me now."

"Best he not find you," Rye said. "The deputy will take

you back to my place. Can live there till the stage comes."

Renee smiled. "You are kind, monsieur," she said, coming to her feet. "I will go there now and rest."

The lawman nodded and motioned to Burke, his own thoughts on Grissom. As the deputy led the woman off down the hallway, he moved for the door.

"I'll be looking for Grissom," he called over his shoulder. Not waiting for any protests or comments from Burke as to the danger of doing such alone, he stepped out into the street and turned for the saloons at its upper end.

It was drawing close to noon. The sun was hot, and there was no one to be seen, but Rye was conscious of the attention of several men inside the Bluebird as he passed, of Wolcott once again in his doorway looking on, and of faces in the upper windows of the Parisian all turned to him.

That's where he'd go first, the lawman decided. Grissom could be there looking for Renee. Besides, it would be a pleasure to give Lefore back that measure of manhandling the saloon keeper had coming.

Reaching the saloon, Rye shouldered roughly past two men just emerging. Ignoring their grumbling protests, he entered. Lefore was behind his small bar, while a half a dozen patrons in company with a like number of women were scattered about on the chairs in the room.

"Looking for Grissom—he here?" the lawman asked in a hard voice.

Lefore's brows lifted, and all conversation in the area ceased. Rye could feel the resentment toward him begin to build instantly. Ignoring it, he kept his grim attention on Lefore while he waited for an answer to his demand.

"Well?" he prompted impatiently.

Lefore shrugged. "Ain't seen him since this morning. Was here most all night."

The lawman considered that in the deep hush for several moments. Then, "That had better be the truth, Lefore," he snapped. "I find out different I'll be back. Got a private score to settle with you, and I'm looking for a good reason to start."

"Score? What for? I sure ain't—"

"Let it ride for now," Rye cut in harshly. It was best to not mention Renee and the fact that he'd had a visit from her, or where she presently was. For her own sake she should remain hidden for the time.

"Don't know what you're talking about!" Lefore protested as the marshal wheeled and headed for the door.

"It'll keep," Rye shot back, and continued on to the street.

The Kansas City—he'd look there next for Grissom. It was a likely place; if he did not turn up the gunman there, he'd go then to the Palo Duro. Crossing over, shoulders a hard, straight line, features set, he walked through the open doorway of the saloon. The place was enjoying the patronage of a dozen or so men at that midday hour, and he strode to where Reno was slouched in a chair at the end of the bar.

"I'm looking for Will Grissom," he said. "He in here somewhere?"

Phil Reno, slightly drunk, raised a hand and waved it at the men ranged along the counter.

"You see them, you lousy tin star?" he shouted in a thick voice. "They're pulling out—leaving—and they claim they ain't coming back—and it's all on account of you! You're killing my business!"

"Grissom—where is he?" Rye cut in sharply as he hung on to his temper. He had no time to straighten Phil Reno out; if he didn't find Grissom soon, word of his search for the gunman would precede him, and the man could become suspicious of the cause, mount up and take hurried leave.

"Hell, I don't know! Go look in his shack out back. Could be there," Reno said, pouring himself another drink.

"Which one's his?"

"First one—first one on the left. What're you looking for him for?"

The lawman, making no reply, moved off at once, crossing the saloon to its rear wall and the door near its center. Opening the panel, he stepped out onto a small landing. The shack, first one to the left, was no more than a dozen strides away. Giving the pistol on his hip a touch to reassure himself of its presence, the marshal came off the platform and walked quickly to the entrance to the old structure. Pausing briefly just outside, Rye drew his pistol and stepped through the opening.

Grissom, sprawled on a cot placed against the wall of the single barren room, lunged to his feet, hand reaching for the holstered weapon hanging from the back of a chair.

"Don't," the lawman warned, his gun leveled.

Grissom lowered his arm, stared at Rye. "What the hell do you want?"

"Talk," Rye answered, moving out of the open doorway. His back was to it and therefore a target for anyone coming onto the scene who might decide to seize the chance to make himself a local hero by cutting down a hated lawman.

"Talk? You and me ain't got nothing to talk about," the gunman said.

"Expect we have," Rye said in a savage tone. "Six murdered soldiers and a box with two hundred thousand dollars in brand-new double eagles!"

Grissom recoiled slightly, and then shook his head. "I don't know nothing about it."

"The hell you don't! You spent one of those double eagles—gave it to a woman at the Parisian!"

Grissom's eyes blazed. "That stinking— I told her not to—" he exploded, and quickly caught himself. "I won that gold piece in a poker game. Don't know who the bird was, but—"

"You're a poor liar, Grissom," the lawman broke in quietly. "I know better. You've got more of those coins— your share of the deal—and you're holding off till things blow over before you start using them. That was the agreement with your partners."

Rye was shooting in the dark, he knew, but he'd been around long enough to have encountered similar situations, and was familiar with the usual arrangement.

"I don't know nothing about it," Grissom declared stubbornly.

The gunman's eyes had narrowed, and a sort of grayness now colored the skin of his face. His mouth was a tight line, and he glanced once or twice at the pistol hanging from the chair while the lawman was speaking, as if calculating his chances to grab it and fight his way out of the shack.

"I've got you cold," Rye said, continuing to run his bluff. "I'm locking you up with my deputy standing guard at the door, then I'm coming back here and take this shack down board by board until I find the rest of the gold. I can promise you one thing, Grissom, you'll swing for your part in that ambush—for the murders of six men."

The gunman was silent for several moments, and then a slyness came into his eyes.

"I reckon not," he drawled. "You're maybe a big, hard-case lawman, but you sure stubbed your toe this time! He ain't taking me nowheres, is he, Jack?"

A smile parted Rye's lips. "You expecting me to swallow that old dodge, Grissom? I'm not about to look around."

"No need, Marshal," a voice said from the doorway. "I'm here—and my gun's pointed right at your head!"

CHAPTER 18

Jack . . . Jack Turner—Grissom's partner. Rye swore bit-
terly. He had expected the word of his search for the gunman to spread, and someone hurry to warn the man, so he
had moved fast himself, hoping to find Grissom first. He
had succeeded in that—but he had not figured on Jack
Turner's taking a hand in the matter.

Grinning, Will Grissom reached for his gun belt and
strapped it on. "He's on to us, Jack—knows about them
soldiers and the gold, the whole thing. Just keep your iron
on him while I go get the horses. Then we'll take this high
and mighty tin-badge marshal out to the brakes and get
rid of him. Been wanting to do that right along, but
Delano and them was scared it'd raise a big stink. Ain't
nothing else we can do now."

Turner, moving in closer, pressed the muzzle of his pistol into Rye's back. "All right, but don't go stopping by
the Kansas City for no drink. I ain't comfortable, standing
here like this holding him. He's plenty tricky and I ain't
sure—"

"Just you keep your iron jammed into his backbone,"
Grissom said, taking the marshal's pistol and tossing it
onto the cot. "I won't be gone more'n ten maybe fifteen
minutes."

Rye felt the pressure of Jack Turner's weapon slack off

as the man turned slightly to face Grissom, who was moving through the doorway.

"Hell, that's a long time, Will! You stay here and keep him quiet, and I'll go get—"

Turner never finished his suggestion. Rye, always sharply alert at such critical moments for an opportunity to reverse a desperate situation, whirled. The motion knocked Turner's gun aside, sent the outlaw stumbling back against the wall near the doorway.

"Damn it to hell!" Jack yelled as Rye threw himself to one side and snatched up his pistol from the cot.

Grissom, caught by Turner's startled shout, spun. He whipped up his weapon, fired hastily. The bullet intended for Rye struck Turner just as he righted himself and lunged for the lawman. Jack, propelled further by the impact of the heavy bullet at such close range, fell into Rye, and together they went down. Struggling to get free, the lawman had a glimpse of Will Grissom as he pivoted, darted through the doorway and headed in the direction of the adjacent Palo Duro Saloon.

Pushing the lifeless Turner aside, the marshal came to his feet and hurried into the yard. Turning right, he expected to see Grissom going after his horse; instead he had a fleeting look of the outlaw just disappearing into the back entrance to the Palo Duro.

Rye broke into a hard run while his mind sought to piece together what he had learned. That Grissom had been in on the ambush was certain. Jack Turner had also been a part of it. Was Ben Delano also a member of the party? Will Grissom had headed straight for Delano as if to warn the man. Such would make it appear so.

The lawman reached the saloon, slowed and came to a

halt outside the door. It would be foolhardy to jerk open the panel and go rushing in; Grissom could be waiting for him. Swiping at the sweat on his forehead that was misting his eyes, the lawman glanced about, saw that the gunshot had drawn no attention or possible interference. Satisfied, he stepped in close to the wall, reached for the doorknob and gave it a turn. When the lock released, the lawman, weapon ready, yanked the panel open.

There was no blast of gunfire. Rye, allowing a dozen heartbeats to pass, assuring himself that the gunman was not just holding off and waiting, ducked low to make of himself a difficult target nevertheless, and plunged into the building.

It was a hallway. Doubtless it led to the main part of the saloon. Moving fast, Rye covered the corridor's length and cautiously drew back a second door; hesitating briefly again, he entered the main room.

There were not many patrons—six or seven—to be seen. Delano and Mada Fremont were at a table near the end of the bar, and both viewed him, as did the customers and the bartender, with cold indifference.

"Grissom—where is he?" Rye demanded, breathing hard from running. "Followed him in here, so don't tell me you haven't seen him."

Delano was calm, unperturbed as usual, and was putting up a good front for a man fearing to be found out as a killer and a thief. He shrugged.

"Don't intend to," he said. "Come through here, went on out. What're you—"

Rye didn't wait to hear the rest of the saloon keeper's question, but hurried on without any reply. For the time being he would give the probability of Ben Delano's

being a party to the ambush of the army wagon no further thought; he would look into that later. Will Grissom
was his immediate object.

He reached the Palo Duro's swinging doors, aware now
that most of the saloon's patrons had left their tables and
places at the bar and were trailing after him, anticipating,
no doubt, the dramatic violence of a shoot-out.

Pushing through the batwings, Rye threw his glance
quickly about. Grissom was climbing the back steps of
Frank Wolcott's General Store. The lawman snapped a
hasty shot at the gunman.

"Grissom! Hold it there!"

The man paused, but only for an instant. Then,
hunched low, he crossed the landing at the rear of the
store, pulled open the screen door and disappeared inside.

Cursing, Rye ran on. There were several persons in the
street now, drawn by the commotion, and while he knew
that a gunshot ordinarily would attract little attention in
the settlement, things being as they were, his presence
had brought about a change. Now the sound of a shot
could mean that the new marshal had killed another man
—or that he himself had been cut down.

The warning he'd fired at Will Grissom aroused Aaron
Burke. Rye saw the deputy, shotgun in his hands, rush
out into the open and look questioningly in the direction
of Wolcott's.

"The front door!" the lawman yelled. "It's Grissom—
stop him!"

Burke nodded and began to move toward the general
store. Rye, at a trot, reached the rear of the place,
climbed the steps two at a time and halted a bit to the
left of the door, again wary of entering any building with-

out first making certain he was not walking head-on into a bullet. Keeping well out of the line of fire, Rye pulled back the screened panel, hearing as he did the pound of boot heels on the bare wood floor of the store.

Grissom was running through the building, as he had the Palo Duro, hoping desperately to reach a horse—any horse—on which he could make an escape. Abruptly the thundering blast of a gunshot inside the store drowned out all else. The thought *Grissom's killed Wolcott* went through the lawman's mind as he dodged through the opening into the building, which was crowded with counters and boxes of merchandise.

Rye saw Grissom in that moment. The gunman was at the front door, one hand clutching the framework as he sought to keep from falling. A dark stain was spreading across his back. *Grissom* had been shot—not Wolcott! The storekeeper, realizing the gunman had committed some breach of law, and apparently switching sides, had shot Grissom to stop his flight from—

"Here's a bullet for *you*, Marshal!" Frank Wolcott yelled suddenly, rising from behind the counter to Rye's left.

The lawman endeavored to spin away as Wolcott triggered the weapon in his hand. He was a fraction of a second too late. The bullet drove into his arm, rocked him backward. But the shocking blow of the slug slowed him only momentarily. As Wolcott, dark eyes bright, features distorted with hate, moved in for a second shot, Rye sent a bullet into the man. Wolcott paused in mid-step, pivoted slowly and fell, overturning a stack of boxes as he did.

Rye, sagging against one of the counters, drew himself

unsteadily erect and looked at his wounded arm. It was bleeding freely, but he ignored it and crossed to where the storekeeper lay. He needed to talk to the man, ask questions, find out why he had shot Grissom, and then turned on *him*. Was he a party to the ambush also?

He would get no answers from Frank Wolcott. The owner of the general store was dead. Rye, holstering his weapon, drew his bandanna from a pocket. Pressing it to the wound in his arm, he swore raggedly. With Grissom and now Wolcott both dead, he was back to the beginning insofar as the murders and theft of the double eagles were concerned.

"Marshal—you all right in there?" It was Burke.

"All right," the lawman replied, and moved to the door. Stepping out onto the landing, he looked down at Grissom sprawled near its edge. Beyond the deputy, kneeling beside the gunman, people were gathering in the street, Lefore and Delano among them.

"Wolcott's dead—what about Grissom?" Rye asked.

"Not yet, but he sure ain't got long. Bullet of yours hit him right between the shoulders."

"Wasn't me—was Wolcott."

"Wolcott? Why—"

"Can't answer that. He shot Grissom, then turned his gun on me. Got me to wondering about things. If we can keep Grissom alive for a bit, maybe we can get the straight of it from him."

The deputy got to his feet, walked down the steps into the crowd. "Any of you got a bottle of whiskey on you? We're needing it."

A man standing next to Lefore said, "Sure, but I ain't about to give it to no damn tin star."

His words broke off into a gasp as Burke rammed the muzzle of his shotgun into the man's belly, clubbed him solidly on the side of the head with the weapon's butt.

As the man went down, the deputy took the half empty bottle from his hands, turned, and retraced his steps to Grissom's side. Kneeling again, he raised the gunman's head and forced a drink down his throat. Rye, surprised and pleased at Aaron Burke's decisive action, hunched beside the deputy and put his attention on Will Grissom's slack features. But before he could speak, the deputy drew back frowning.

"Hell, Marshal, you been shot!"

Rye shook his head. "Nothing much—bullet got me in the thick of my arm."

"Maybe it ain't much," Burke said, "but you're sure bleeding like a stuck hog." Twisting about to again face the crowd, he called out, "Zeke, go get the Mueller girl. Tell her the marshal's been shot, needs doctoring."

Zeke, a tall, grizzled man in a linsey-woolsey shirt and new overalls, drew up stiffly. "Hell, I ain't your toting-boy! You want her, you get her."

Burke allowed Grissom's head to rest again on the floor of the store landing. Taking the shotgun in hand once more, he got to his feet.

"Zeke, you wanting a little of what I give Gabe?" he demanded coldly. "I'm the deputy here for the marshal, and when he's hurt I'm in charge. Now, you get the hell over there after that girl!"

Zeke hesitated, then took a quick look at Gabe, now sitting on the ground, legs outstretched before him as he rubbed at the side of his head. Wheeling, he started for the Bluebird at a run.

Rye, smiling approvingly at Burke, turned back to Grissom. Removing his hand from the bandanna compress, he slipped it under the outlaw's head, raised it slightly.

"Will, you're dying. Wolcott's bullet's finished you off. Want to ask you a couple of questions."

The gunman's eyes fluttered open, then closed as the midday sun struck them full on. Immediately, Aaron Burke pulled off his hat and held it over the gunman's face, shading it. Grissom's eyes opened again.

"Who—who're you?"

"The marshal . . . was Wolcott in on that ambush with you and Turner?"

"Yeh. Hired me and Jack and a couple of drifters to help him do it."

Wolcott! The information that the storekeeper was the man leading the ambush rocked the lawman. "Paid you off with some of the double eagles, told you not to spend them for a time."

The gunman nodded weakly. "Frank was going busted here in the store. Reason he rigged up the ambush. Him and a soldier—lieutenant—a nephew—I recollect—up Nevada way."

That explained it. The insider at the mint had been the lieutenant who turned back. He had advised Wolcott of when and where the army wagon with its shipment of gold coins could be expected, and thus allowed the storekeeper time to plan the ambush. Chances were the lieutenant would be showing up to claim his share of the double eagles before long.

"Why did Wolcott shoot you?"

"Told him I'd had to give out one of the coins, that you had it all figured out—was after me. Frank went sort of

looney. Said I'd ruined everything. Told me to run. Said
he'd take care of you. When I did, he shot me."

"And when I showed up he tried to kill me," Rye
added. "Probably was going to say that you and I shot it
out and we both went down."

Rye felt a hand on his arm and glanced around. It was
the Mueller girl. She had a small bag in which were rolls
of bandages, bottles of medicine, cotton and the like.

"Can let that go till later," he said. Will Grissom didn't
have many more minutes left, and there were still questions to be asked and answered.

"No," the girl said firmly, "it is best now."

The marshal did not relent, came back to Grissom.
"Will, where is the gold? Where did Wolcott hide it?"

The outlaw opened his eyes with an effort. "Box—under
the floor—back room. Can I have—another shot of that
whiskey?"

Rye nodded to Burke, who held the bottle to the gunman's lips, and allowed him to drink. When he'd had
enough, Grissom sank back wearily.

"Guess it was you that drove the wagon into the barn
at the old Montgomery place, and then set it a'fire," the
deputy said, taking up the questioning.

"Yeh—me and Frank. He was—afraid the marshal—
would find something—"

The lawman settled back, allowed the Mueller girl to
begin dressing the wound in his arm. To learn that Wolcott had been the leader in the ambush had been a surprise. He had thought the storekeeper's continual insist-
ence that he leave town had been because he was against
the re-establishment of the law and the resultant destruc-
tion of the monopoly the council was enjoying.

It appeared now that there was more to it; Wolcott realized that his part in the murders and theft was about to be found out, and he was doing everything possible to prevent it. But it was all finished now. All that remained was to locate the double eagles and have them on hand and ready to turn over to the army detail when it arrived. It would not all be there. They likely could recover that which had been given by Wolcott to Grissom and Jack Turner when they searched their quarters, but the two drifters . . . Rye frowned—without any names it would be impossible—.

"Grissom," he said, bending quickly over the gunman, "those drifters that were with you—tell me their names."

Aaron Burke shook his head. "He can't tell you nothing, Marshal. He's dead."

The lawman shrugged. Wolcott probably hadn't paid them much, so he reckoned it wasn't too important. If the Army figured it was, it would be up to them to track the pair down.

He looked around. The Mueller girl had finished bandaging his arm, after pouring some kind of burning liquid directly into the hole that the bullet—which had missed the bone and passed on through—had made.

"Obliged to you," he said when she drew back. The girl smiled, began to collect her stock of medical items.

"Expect you're all wondering just what this was all about," he heard Burke say to the crowd, and then listened quietly as the deputy went ahead with a brief summary that concluded with the report: "The marshal got himself winged doing it. It ain't bad, but he's going to have a mighty sore arm for a while."

Vic Lefore, standing at the edge of the crowd with Delano, laughed. "I guess that means you're going to be strutting around acting real big with that star on your vest."

"You're right, Vic," Burke replied in a hard voice, fixing the saloon keeper with a cold stare. "And if you're thinking that's funny you best change your thinking real fast! I'm the law here now that the marshal's bunged up, and you had all better get this straight—there ain't nothing changed!

"Things are a'going on just the same as if the marshal was still running this town, and any man—and that sure includes you, Vic—that ain't doing according to the law is going to jail, or getting blasted to hell with this here shotgun of mine if he argues the point. I reckon I've made myself plain."

There was a long hush, and then, as the gathering began to break up, Jeremiah Potter said, "You dang sure have, Aaron, and I want you to know I'm all for you—and I expect there's plenty others that'll feel the same."

"I'm hoping so," the deputy said. "And I'm hoping you and some of the rest'll help me get the word out—that this town's going to be like it was a time ago—and see if we can't start folks to moving back."

"Can count on me," Potter said, and turned to Rye. "What about you, Marshal? You aim to hang around until the new sheriff gets here?"

Rye glanced at Aaron Burke standing square-shouldered and firm, the double-barrel hanging in the crook of an arm as he looked out over the dispersing crowd. The deputy had found himself, there was no doubt of that.

L25

"I'll be around for a spell, I expect, but I won't be waiting for a new sheriff. The way I see it, you've already got one there in Aaron, and I'll be sending a letter to the governor telling him so."